IMMORTAL

UNRAVELED

EMMA SHELFORD

UNRAVELED

Copyright © 2021 Emma Shelford
Cover design by Deranged Doctor Design

www.emmashelford.com

ISBN: 978-1989677315 (paperback)
ISBN: 978-1989677285 (ebook)

First edition: April 2021

DEDICATION

To Academie Duello for the inspiration
and
to Marli, who took "being a good sport" to a whole new level

CHAPTER I

The classroom aisle spins disconcertingly. I shouldn't have had that last beer.

I wobble to the front and slowly turn to the class to avoid the room spinning around me. This is the third week of the January term, and I've managed to stay sober for every class until today. But early this morning, in the silence of my lonely apartment, memories hit me hard.

The students stare at me. Some look concerned, some giggle behind their hands, and others look half-asleep. I run my hands through my black hair, cut short for the twenty-first century, and try to pull myself together for a lecture about Geoffrey Chaucer. I give up almost immediately.

"As you might have guessed, I'm deeply intoxicated right now. My wife died recently, and it turns out alcohol is a passable way to dull the pain." I see looks of sympathy passed between students and wave my hand. "You needn't concern yourself, it shouldn't matter to you. Now, you may, of course, run to the dean and report my abysmal behavior." I prop myself against the desk to avoid swaying. "Or, we can have a little fun today. I'll pull out my best acting skills, and we can pretend you're meeting characters from literature in your favorite bar. Drunken characters, obviously."

A titter travels through the class. I raise my eyebrow.

"Consensus? You may leave now if you wish."

No one moves, and I smile.

"All right, hit me with a character. Your choice."

The first student cautiously puts up her hand, and I wave to indicate she should speak.

"What about Puck from Shakespeare's Midsummer's Night Dream?"

I close my eyes and prepare myself for the role. The class is breathless, waiting to see what I will do. I open my eyes and give the student a mischievous grin.

"Lady, thou spy the rub; I am that merry drinker in the pub. I jest to Oberon, and make him smile, when I a fat and drunken lout beguile, snorting in likeness of a sodden pig."

The class snickers, but I'm not done yet. I throw my arms out for dramatic effect.

"And sometime spin I in an alehouse jig, in very likeness of a girlish slip; and, when I drink, onto my tongue I sip, and from my comely hands pour I the ale. The wisest drunk, telling the saddest tale, sometime for wise woman mistaketh me; then pour I more ale, down topples he, and 'Puck' he cries, and falls onto the straw; and then the tavern bursts into guffaws; and waxen in their mirth, and neeze, and swear, a merrier hour was never wasted there."

It's my own take on a speech by Puck, and certainly not my finest work, but today I'm not at my finest. The students don't seem to mind. They clap with shouts of laughter, and I grace them with a sweeping bow that nearly topples me over.

After that, student hands rise with alacrity, and I indulge them all. Brooding Heathcliff, intellectual Sherlock Holmes, witty Elizabeth Bennet, even wise yet hilariously sodden Gandalf. Even if I hadn't had centuries of deception and changes of persona to draw upon, I have had my fair share of acting jobs. I avoid fame—it's difficult to slip away unnoticed when my lack of aging threatens to unravel my deceptions— but in the eras before mass media, it was a safe enough profession. Shakespeare was a historical figure I knew well, after a season of acting at the Globe. The bastard still owes me twelve shillings, but it's hard to collect from a dead debtor.

When the hour is up, I raise my hand for quiet. Laughter subsides, and all eyes are on me.

2

"All of that is testable, of course," I say. The students stare at me, slack-jawed. I chuckle. "Only joking. I probably won't remember any of this. You're free to go. Go on, bugger off."

There's a tremendous rustling as students pack their backpacks and shuffle to the door. I rub my forehead and wince. The alcohol is wearing off already, and the pain of Minnie's loss slams into my chest like a sharpened lance in my vulnerable state.

It's Friday, and I have only one more class. I could plead illness and leave early for the mountains. The dean has been much more lenient since Minnie's passing, despite my former probation from a lack of attendance. The leniency won't last forever, but I'll take advantage of it today.

"Dr. Lytton?"

The soft voice of one of my students gives me pause. Is her name Christine, or perhaps Crystal? I can't remember. I've stumbled through this term in a fog.

"Yes?" I sling my satchel over my shoulder to give a clear impression that I won't stay for a long chat. I need to get out of here. The mountains will take away the unbearable squeeze of my heart.

"My grandmother's house caught fire last week," she says with hesitation. "I've been helping out, and now I'm behind on my classwork. Can I have an extension?"

I wave my hand.

"Yes, that's fine." At the sight of her drooping lauvan, I sigh. Clearly, my response wasn't as thoughtful as it could have been. "Ask at the office for a note for your other classes."

"Thanks, Dr. Lytton."

She scurries off, and I follow her to the lecture hall door. I would feel badly that I wasn't as sympathetic as I should have been, but my other feelings overwhelm me. I easily justify the brush-off—if I don't fulfill my crucial duties at the mountain, then I'm not honoring Minnie's sacrifice—but the niggling guilt remains.

I shake my head impatiently. The mountains call.

The admin gives me a baleful glance when I inform him of my illness and imminent departure, but evidently my status as grief-ridden mourner holds firm, for he doesn't question me. Outside, I find a quiet place to transform into a merlin falcon. I was too drunk to drive this morning, so I flew instead.

Strong wings lift me from the ground, and I let the wind blow away my malaise. Soon, I will be at the mountains. Soon, I will be performing my duties. I flap my wings harder, annoyed by their weight. Ever since I assumed my fundamental mantle, flying has been more difficult. I suppose my increased affinity for earth doesn't mix well with soaring in the air, but I persevere. Flying is an activity I won't give up easily.

I circle down to my apartment building, eager to pack for my weekend trip. I don't aim for my old ninth floor balcony this time. I switched apartments last month when a ground floor suite became vacant. It was hard to sleep separated from the earth. Although some brown strands slither over the concrete of the building, it's not enough for comfort. The new suite has the bonus of fewer reminders of Minnie.

Familiar lauvan hangs off my doorknob. I sigh and push the door open. Someone stirs inside.

"What are you doing here, Jen?" I say in a tired voice.

Jennifer Chan, one of my oldest and most stalwart friends, peers at me in concern from the hallway.

"I had the day off today since I just came back from a job.

4

Wayne called me and said you left early, so I thought I'd meet you here." She waves at the door behind me, and her long black hair swishes. "And you never lock your door."

My mouth twitches. My lack of locks never ceases to annoy Jen, but I don't have anything worth stealing that isn't already protected within the suite.

"I'm not staying long. What did you want to see me about?"

I drop my satchel on the floor and move to the kitchen. I'll need food that is quick and doesn't require cooking. I'll be busy for most of the weekend, and heating food will only take time.

My fridge is empty except for a half case of beer, and I slam the door in disgust. My cupboards are similarly sparse, and I resign myself to a stop at the grocery store before my mountain trek. Jen leans against the counter and crosses her arms.

"Where are you going?" she asks.

"North," I say, but Jen must understand my terse answer, for she frowns.

"Again? Are you staying the whole weekend? I don't know, Merry, is that healthy? Do you really need to spend that long in the other plane?"

I close the cupboard door and squeeze past Jen into the hallway. A closet at the end vomits out a folded tarp, shoved in there from last weekend. It smells faintly musty—I must have put it away damp—but I throw it toward the front door anyway.

"I'm the earth fundamental," I say, then I sigh.

Jen and the others don't understand, not really. I have a sacred duty to uphold now that the mantle of earth power has been placed upon me. I have a responsibility to the elementals, to the world, and to Minnie's memory. I can't squander that by lazing around my apartment and drinking beers with my friends, even if I wanted to. And I don't, not really, not now.

5

That lighter part of me died with Minnie.

"It's an important job," I continue. "And no one can do it but me."

I sweep past Jen on the way to my bedroom for a blanket, but Jen grabs my hand and forces me to stop.

"I'm worried about you." She bites her lips and stares at me with her expressive brown eyes. "I thought the other fundamentals said you could live your human life as well. Why the ultra-dedication?"

Jen's warm hand in mine briefly breaks through my focus. I stare at our clasped hands, and words escape me without my consent.

"It's easier there," I say quietly. "I don't feel as much. You'd be surprised how physical grief is."

Jen's breath hitches.

"Oh, Merry." She releases my hand then wraps her arms around my body. "I'm sorry. I wish there were more I could do to help."

"You're doing it," I whisper into her hair. A stab of longing for Minnie's arms instead of Jen's punches me in the gut, and I hold my breath until the sensation passes. I thought I would be used to grief by now, after centuries of it, but even the hope that Minnie might come back to me one day isn't enough to soothe my anguish.

I don't allow myself to savor the human contact for long. I have things to do, and if I don't break away from Jen's embrace now, I might never let her go.

"I'll be back Sunday evening," I tell Jen and avoid her compassionate eyes by entering my bedroom. After retrieving my blanket, I return to the hallway. "Don't worry about me too much. This grief isn't anything I haven't felt before. It always passes. Eventually."

"Okay," she says, clearly not willing to press me further.

"Take care of yourself up there. And call me on Sunday."

"I'll try," I say and usher her over the threshold. She leaves with a final worried glance, and I close the door behind her with a sigh. Every minute I waste in this apartment is another minute I'm not in the mountains.

My meager supplies fit in a backpack, and I sling it over my shoulder before exiting my dwelling. In the underground parking of my apartment building, my vehicle waits for me. I ditched the Volkswagen van after Minnie died—it was too sharp a reminder, especially when I purchased it entirely for her—and sprang for a street motorcycle. Jen gave me a raised eyebrow when I first turned up on the bike, because she never approved of my previous two-seater. This was even worse, even with the tiny passenger spot behind the main saddle, but I made no apologies. Minnie isn't there to ride with me, and I rarely want the company of anyone else. A solitary bike was the perfect solution.

The bike kicks to a start with a vicious roar, and I peel out of the parking garage with grim resolution. A quick stop at the grocery store to buy enough food to keep body and soul together, then to the mountains. With any luck, I will be there in under an hour.

Rain patters against the face shield of my helmet, and I groan. This weekend will be cold and wet. It's to be expected in late January, but still not welcome. Luckily, I won't be present in my body for long enough to fully feel the effects of the weather. With a tarp and blanket to keep out the worst of the weather, I will survive. I have more important things to do than pander to my body's whims.

Movement on the sidewalk catches my eye at a red light. An elderly man trips, stumbles, and drops his grocery bag. Bright oranges spill out and roll into the road, and he shuffles to frantically pick up the ones he can reach.

7

It would be a simple matter for me to pull over and help him gather his scattered groceries, but the mountains call me. Helping him would be a five-minute detour, and then I would lose my early advantage at the grocery store, and the after-work crowd would slow me further.

He's doing fine. Almost all the oranges are back in his bag, and only two are left. One rolls to a wobbly stop near my boot, and I stare at it for a moment.

The light turns green. I gently kick the orange to the curb, and the man croaks his thanks. I nod and roar off, a squirming in my gut reminding me that I didn't deserve any thanks. Kicking the fruit was hardly an act of generosity.

But the mountains beckon, and far more crucial tasks await me there. The old man might have bruised fruit, but Earth won't function properly without my help, and he will benefit from that. It will have to be enough.

The grocery store is quiet, as I predicted, and I grab easily eaten food like bread, cheese, and pepperoni. It will do until Sunday evening, especially since I don't feel hunger pangs when I'm in the lauvan network. Before long, my food is safely stowed in the compartment under my seat, and I'm ripping up the highway northward. Seymour and Grouse, two mountains on the North Shore, loom over me with impressive, white-capped peaks, but I follow the highway left toward Cypress. A switchback road loops ever upward, and cornering on the bike brings distinctive pleasure as my knees hover close to the pavement.

A little-used side trail beckons, and I pull over and kill the engine. My bike is small enough to push into the shade of trees and bushes to hide it, then I settle my backpack more securely over my shoulders and strike out into the woods.

The view between trees is spectacular, despite drifting clouds that partly obscure city and steely ocean with ragged

8

streamers of fog. The woods are quiet and still, and even birds have vacated for somewhere warmer and more hospitable. A scent of cold dampness permeates my surroundings, and I breathe deeply to shake off my week of pent-up city dwelling. Living in the floodplains of Vancouver never bothered me before, but since I have become the earth fundamental, I encounter my most peaceful moments in the mountains.

Finally, the promise of water gleams between tree trunks, and I emerge from the woods onto the shores of a small lake, no more than a large pond. A great blue heron gazes at me balefully from across the shallow water. It must deem me not a threat, for it glances away with majestic disdain and carefully walks with skinny long legs to a new section of shoreline. I heave a contented sigh and drop my bag.

"Hello, Minnie," I say quietly. "I'm back."

After Minnie died, I turned her body to dust and instructed the air fundamental to whisk away her ashes to this lake. The Nimue of my youth was the Lady of the Lake. This resting place for her latest incarnation seemed fitting.

I say no more, content to bask in the stillness and peace of the lake, but when memories threaten to overwhelm me, I zip open my backpack and extract the tarp. With a few quick motions, I tie the blue plastic to my usual trees to form a rudimentary shelter, then lay down a rolled mat and my blanket underneath. It's not much, but I have slept in far less hospitable shelters, so it doesn't faze me.

When I'm snugly sequestered in my blanket cocoon, dim light fading from the winter's sky and rain tapping on my tarp, I pull earth strands over myself in a woven sheet of protection. Then, I close my eyes and spread my fingers to grasp earth strands that lie across the surface of the ground. With a sigh, I release my lauvan into the network of threads.

9

CHAPTER II

The world of touch and hearing fades, and my inner eye opens to a completely different world. Formless black is liberally intersected with glowing threads of every color imaginable. Browns of earth strands carpet the featureless ground, and green thread-pillars soar upward in the shapes of trees. In this view, clusters of hibernating animals slumber in invisible burrows, and the lake spreads before me as a calmly undulating mass of blue strands. Almost too far away to see, the city's multitude of colorful lauvan twinkle below.

Now that I know what to look for, the elementals that inhabit this plane are clear to see. Tucked in the brown of the earth, flowing in the blue of water, soaring in the silvery air, and even flickering in an occasional orange fire, elementals shimmer at the edge of my vision. I don't interact with them, and they avoid me, since I am a fundamental with power and influence.

The sensations of my body's heightened emotions are stripped away here. I can view events dispassionately, and it's a tremendous relief. One day, I'll be able to remember Minnie without the crushing weight of grief and hopelessness, but that day is not yet here. Until it arrives, escape into the network is a welcome balm.

I sit in the network for a while, not striving for anything, simply soaking in the sensation. Now that I am the earth fundamental, I am intimately connected to this planet. With patience—I am still new to all this, after all—earth speaks to me. Not in words, of course, but I can sense its ebbs and flows, balances and imbalances, shocking earthquakes, and the slow grind of tectonic plates. When I was a mere half-elemental, the most I could travel in the earth cables was a few hundred kilometers, and my perception was limited. Now, without conscious thought, I can pinpoint where on the globe each earth movement is, and I can travel to it in short order.

It's heady, and if I experienced it while still in my human form, I would be entirely overwhelmed. But in the lauvan network, I am not human and do not have the limitations of a body. The stretching of my strands that happened before I assumed the fundamental mantle allowed me to bear this burden.

I survey the impressions that wash over me, slowly letting them coalesce into intelligible information. A build-up of strands threatens to create a surprise landslide north of here, a stuck tectonic plate thrums with tension near Chile, and an unexpected geyser waits underground in Iceland.

Earth lauvan can become imbalanced for several reasons. Sometimes, the elementals in charge of that region are lax in their duties, and lauvan that should flow smoothly snarl from a lack of diligence. Other times, the clash of different elements need additional care to ensure unity. And sometimes, repeating tangles occur from unknown cycles of nature.

Before I can tackle any of these imbalances, two familiar elementals present themselves in the network. One has auburn strands, the other has threads of a deep loam brown.

"Greetings, Earth," auburn Tremor says in my mind. "We were wondering when we would see you next."

"You missed a dust-up in the Sahara," loam-brown Quake says with glee. "Air elementals were getting very snotty, but we cut them down to size."

"I haven't been able to do much more than occasional check-ins this week," I say. "My human life got in the way. I'm tempted to quit my job and spend more time in the network. This is where the important work happens. I doubt I would be much missed in the physical world."

"We managed without you," Tremor says, her voice soothing. "Your presence alone, whether in this plane or not, takes care of most of the balancing. Without a proper fundamental, the threads of the world tried to fill the void in disastrous ways. With you in the mix, things mostly flow as they should."

"We can handle a lot," Quake says with pride.

"Good," I say. "I'm glad to have you as my seconds. You have both been tremendous guides on this terrifying journey, and it's helpful to have liaisons to the rest of the elementals. Today, there are three trouble spots: a misplaced landslide, a pressure-filled tectonic plate, and an overactive geyser. We need to smooth those over."

I send a mental image of each location to the other two and receive back sensations of confirmation.

"Leave us with the landslide and the geyser," Quake says. "I'll whip those water elementals into shape. But that tectonic plate needs your attention. Better release the pressure now before we get into real trouble. Any longer, and we'd feel aftershocks in the network for days."

"All right," I say, relieved to delegate some of my duties to these capable elementals. "I'll get on it."

Tremor and Quake flit off, Tremor in the direction of the landslide and Quake toward Iceland's geyser. I pour my strands toward the other side of the world.

Faster and faster, I soar over lauvan until the threads are only a colorful smear below. Greens and browns eventually flicker into shades of blue ocean as I glide southward toward Chile and the troublesome plate. It's exhilarating, although the effect is dampened by my inability to feel emotions within my body. Until I spent time in the network, I didn't realize how much emotion depended on a physical state.

I slow when the sensation of the troubled plate grows

stronger. Smears resolve into strands, and I follow a concentration of earth threads along the edge of the plate. Below a cluster of multicolored strands that indicates a town, the snarl is clearly visible. I send a pulse of displeasure into the network, and three elementals answer the summons with guilt pouring off them in waves.

"What happened?" I ask. "How did the plate get into this state?"

"We forgot our duties, fundamental," one elemental answers. "We wished to increase our standing in the elemental plane and so tried a new method of landscape suppression. As you can see, it didn't work."

"Please don't send us into dormancy," another elemental bursts out. "Please. We promise to never neglect our duties again."

I let them simmer in silence for a moment. Soldiers, students, elementals: all respond to a similar knack of holding attention. I've had centuries to perfect my technique.

"I will be lenient," I say slowly. "This one time."

"Thank you," they murmur, their relief washing over me in a flood of gratitude.

"But remember, increase in prestige is achieved through careful adherence to your current duties. You can't skip steps."

I indicate they should leave, and they flit away rapidly, leaving me to my task. I allow myself a moment of annoyance at the three elementals, but I can't stay angry for long. They were acting just how I would if I were a mid-grade elemental. There is only room for responsibility in this plane of existence, but that doesn't mean I can't sympathize with a freethinker.

My strands dive past the colorful small town and deep into the mantle. Earth strands at the plate's edge throb at the entanglement. If I had lungs, I would sigh. It's a messy knot and will take me some time.

13

But this is my duty, and the world has entrusted me with it. It's not like I have anything better to do this weekend.

I flow over the tangle, picking and prodding with my strands and intention the way Tremor and Quake taught me when I first became a fundamental. Both were invaluable teachers, and they earned their places as my trusted advisers.

The knot is tight and large, with pulsing threads that threaten to trap me in their flailing arms, but I dart between them and loosen the tangles. When the snag is halfway unraveled, everything shifts.

I shoot back from the bundle of throbbing threads and peer at it with confusion. What was that?

With a jolt, the strands snap out of their conformation with speedy resolution. In the space of a second, the snarled mess transforms into smoothly flowing strands once more.

If I had a mouth, it would smile. I must have released a lynchpin of sorts, and once that was dealt with, the rest of the tangle had nothing to hold it together. That was a job well done, and quicker than I had expected. Perhaps there isn't much to this fundamental role, after all.

I soar to the surface where lauvan resolve into many colors instead of the predominant brown of the mantle. My conscious glances at the town above the former knot. Instead of the calmly flowing strands of a sleepy town, threads dart around with frenetic energy. I swoop closer, curious about the commotion.

Closer, human lauvan are visible running in frantic directions. Houses that were once covered with earth lauvan from their towering brick construction are now pale piles of minimal strands on the ground. Some pillars of green lie horizontally, and pink strands squirm under one. Clusters of other human lauvan tug at threads to release the pink cluster from the tree trapping it.

I float backward, my mind uneasy. Of course. The tectonic plate must have shifted when I relieved the pressure on its strands. For these poor unfortunates living directly on top of the fault line, they experienced a devastating earthquake.

I float back to my body, allowing the pull of my physical form to drag my elemental strands away from the distraught town. Tremor and Quake wait for me near the chocolate brown strands that outline my body.

"Your tasks are complete?" I ask them.

"Yes," Tremor says, and Quake's strands pulse in agreement. "Fairly simple matters."

"Speak for yourself," Quake says. "My geyser was a whopper."

"An earthquake occurred once I released the pressure on the plate," I say. "A town was greatly affected. Property damage, injuries, many fine trees demolished. What could I have done differently to prevent that?"

Confusion emanates from the two elementals.

"It had to happen," Tremor says eventually. "The balance must be maintained. It is unfortunate, I suppose, but it is the way of things. If you hadn't released the pressure, the later destruction would have been catastrophic instead of merely unpleasant for the humans."

There isn't much to say to this. I know she speaks the truth, even as unease gnaws at my mind.

"Until next time," I say and meld into my body.

I open my eyes with a gasp. The winter sun is low on the horizon, peeking from under threatening clouds piled so thickly that I'm astonished the sun hasn't collapsed from the weight. I'm freezing, my entire body shuddering now that I'm aware of it, and my stomach feels like it's digesting me from the inside.

I think back to the events within the network and my

15

conversation with Tremor and Quake, and any feelings of hunger die when guilt hits me like a punch to the gut. Now that emotions course through my body, physical sensations of guilt and shame nearly overwhelm me. The squirming pink of the trapped child under a fallen tree haunts my inner vision. That was me. I caused that destruction, that fear, that pain.

I clench my fists, breathing heavily. I can't go down that road. Like Tremor said, it was necessary. In causing a little mayhem, I prevented much wider-scale destruction. I can't afford to get squeamish about what I need to do. I have a job, a duty, and I must carry it through, even if it's distasteful. I can't let my weak human nature stop me from fulfilling my fundamental role for the greater good.

It might hurt to consider the squirming pink strands, but it hurts more to ignore Minnie's sacrifice by not performing my fundamental duties admirably.

I swallow the last of my shame and throw back the blanket. When my eyes land on my backpack, I rip it open and shove pepperoni into my waiting mouth. My stomach cramps with hunger pangs from almost two days in the network, and I follow the pepperoni with a bun while I roughly roll my blanket with one hand and push it into my backpack. After a gulp of water and a visit to a nearby tree to relieve myself, I take one last look at Minnie's placid lake and turn to the trail and my hidden bike.

It's dark by the time I enter my floor-level apartment, and my stomach is gnawing at me again. I'm still chilled to the bone, and my ride through driving rain in only a leather jacket didn't help. I hang my jacket to drip in the hallway and jump

16

into a scalding hot shower that only marginally helps.

The fridge is still empty, and I slam it shut before zipping open my backpack and feeling around for the remains of my food. My hunk of cheese won't get me far, but I have no desire to leave the apartment again until morning. I have gone to bed on a much emptier stomach before. I know how to ignore the pangs of my body.

The apartment is too quiet, and my thoughts drift inevitably to Minnie. After feeling nothing all weekend, my emotions are raw and overwhelming. My shoulders rise and my head hunches down as if to protect myself, but I can't prevent pain that comes from the inside. I wish I could spend all my time in the network, but the other fundamentals insist that I continue my human life so that my body is properly maintained. Since I can't survive as an elemental alone, taking care of myself is paramount.

But that doesn't mean I can't numb the anguish. I consider the case of beer cooling in my fridge, then sigh. My students excused me for one day's intoxication, but if I repeat that fiasco, I doubt I would get so lucky again. Without my work as an instructor at the university, what would I do all day? It's a decent distraction if I must hang around in this body of flesh.

A knock interrupts my surly musings, and I stomp to the front door and swing it open. My friend Alejandro stands on the threshold, and my eyes are drawn to the bag of Thai takeout in his hand. My stomach growls loudly.

"Come in," I say. Although I can't deny my attraction to the delicious scent of noodles, I don't want company this evening, and my manner is decidedly grumpy.

Alejandro gives me a look, as if he sees my inner conundrum, but he enters the apartment and slips off his shoes.

"You're always hungry on Sundays. Jen says you don't eat properly on the mountain."

"What, is she my mother now?" I mutter and follow Alejandro into the main room. He glances at me but otherwise ignores my churlish comment. I dip into the kitchen and return with plates, spoons, and forks, and Alejandro wordlessly accepts a set. He rips open the bag, and I descend on the containers within.

Once we have eaten our fill in silence, I sit back and sigh.

"Thanks, Alejandro. That was good."

"Are you ready to talk about what happened this weekend?"

I frown and stare at Alejandro. He gazes back calmly.

"What do you want to know? I went to the mountains, like I always do these days, and plugged into the network. I did my fundamental job, then I came back. There's nothing else to tell."

"But what is your fundamental job? You haven't told anyone about it. Is it difficult? Can you manage? Are the other elementals treating you with respect despite your half-elemental status? What's it like?"

I chase an errant red pepper on my plate with my spoon for something to focus on, although I'm too full to eat it.

"I fix lauvan that need to be fixed. That's all. It's really quite dull, I promise you."

My mind wanders to the squirming pink cluster and frantic threads in the Chilean town, and I swallow my distaste. I'm doing the right thing, I know I am—despite the cost of my actions—but I have no desire to discuss the details of my weekend with Alejandro. I don't need to see horror or disgust on his face. Alejandro is always concerned about doing the right thing, and the nuances of harming a small number of people for the greater good would be lost on him.

But my deception rankles. I don't like keeping things from my friends. The actions of my fundamental role only serve to underline the differences between us. I'm not one of them

18

anymore, not entirely, and it's difficult to justify my necessary actions to those who are not of my new world.

Alejandro stares at me for a moment longer, but he must sense that I am finished talking, because he sighs and doesn't press further.

"I had an idea," he says by way of changing the subject. "Well, Wayne and I did. He was saying how lucky he feels to have met Anna."

"They're still going strong, are they?"

"Seems like it. But he wasn't having much luck dating before her. It's hard to meet people once you're in the rut of work."

I've never found it difficult, but I can understand how others might.

"So, what's your idea?"

"What if I started an outdoor adventure business?" Alejandro's eyes light up with his new notion. "For single people. We would host hiking adventures in the mountains, weekend getaways. It would be great for getting to know others when they're real. In the face of adversity and all that." He pauses. "I hate to see people be lonely only because they don't have the opportunity to connect."

I smile.

"That sounds like you. You'll find any way to help others."

"I was hoping you could help out," he says. "I want to bounce ideas off you, and I'll need to find sponsorship or a loan of some sort to get going."

I'm shaking my head before Alejandro finishes speaking.

"I have too much on my plate right now to find sponsors. I'm sorry, but between work and my fundamental duties, I'm swamped." I cast about for something to say at the sight of Alejandro's crestfallen face. "I'm sure you'll do splendidly. You'll figure it out. But I'm always up for discussing details.

I'm an excellent manager."

Alejandro chuckles.

"None of the work and all of the credit? That sounds like a role you're well suited for."

Once Alejandro departs, my eyelids can barely stay open after an exhausting weekend in the mountains and a generous helping of takeout. Alejandro's passion for helping others is the last thing that drifts through my mind as I fall asleep.

CHAPTER III
Dreaming

Familiar barnyard scents of dusty hay and fresh dung fill my nostrils. Two children haul at the bridle of a stubborn donkey while another yells in a high-pitched voice from his perch on the fence. Their goal is clear—a slightly bent plow that has seen better days waits in a nearby field—but the donkey is adamant in its refusal to move.

I chuckle and vault over the fence.

"Having fun?" I ask.

The children stop yanking at the reins, and the older girl sighs. She can't have seen more than ten summers, but few of the children here know their true age. She's old enough to clean her face in the mornings, but young enough to miss the back of her neck.

"He just won't go," she says with a glare at the donkey, who stares back with mournful eyes from underneath long lashes.

I grab the donkey's bridle in one hand and with the other pretend to stroke the animal's head while I tease its strands.

"Stop giving the children a hard time," I say quietly to the animal. "Plow that field, and I expect they'll find a carrot for you somewhere."

With a snort, the donkey shakes its head. I let go and wave at the children to try again. The girl frowns at me, but the younger boy beside her tugs the reins. The donkey steps placidly forward.

"You did it, Mikuláš," the boy whoops. "Finally, he's moving."

I rub the boy's head and climb out of the pen.

"Don't forget that carrot," I whisper to the smaller boy on the fence. "Donkey will need it after his hard work."

The boy puffs his tiny chest with importance. He jumps with an unsteady landing onto hard-packed dirt then races toward the storehouse.

I continue toward my destination while I survey the farm. At least twenty children live here, and those who are old enough to contribute do so. They are victims of the Black Death, not from contracting the disease themselves, but from their parents dying from it. Arnost, the friend I made after returning from Africa after the worst of the plague had passed, has made it his mission to collect and care for these orphans. Somehow, he wrangled me into helping.

I don't mind. It's a way to pass the time, and Arnost is a good companion. The children, in typical youthful fashion, range from sweet to irritating and back to sweet, most within the same day. Occasionally, one will remind me of my own lost son and daughters, and the pang of remembrance twists my heart.

The youngest children, still too tiny to toddle around on their own, are cared for by a village woman we hired. She's young but competent, and she has taken it upon herself to teach the elder children how to prepare meals. Arnost, although he won't say it aloud, views her as a treasure. He's caught between her sharp tongue and gentle smile, and I'm amused by their slowly blossoming romance.

We don't have much on this tiny farm. But between crops the children plant, the animals they tend, and an influx of funds that Arnost and I liberate from distant gentry, we survive.

I find Arnost in a field behind the cottage, the collar of his shirt untied and his hat pushed up on his sweaty forehead. He shovels muck from the animals in rows along a recently plowed field. Three youngsters work diligently behind him, one with a pitchfork to stir in the manure and two smaller ones who poke seeds into the ground.

"Shall I prepare the horses?" I call out when I'm in earshot. Arnost straightens his back and wipes his forehead with a sleeve.

"Yes," he replies. "I'll finish this row, then I'll be ready."

The children glance at each other, but Arnost sees their nervous looks. He smiles broadly.

"Don't worry, children. Mikuláš is an excellent fighter, and I can take care of myself. We will all eat meat tonight, God willing."

The little girl planting seeds gasps with delight. Arnost chuckles then bends to his task once more.

I turn my steps to the barn. By the time I've cinched saddles around our two steeds, Arnost appears wearing a long, undyed cape and a wide-brimmed hat. He tosses me my own cape and hat.

"To the narrowing near Rudná?" he says.

"It's a long ride," I warn.

"We can't be too close. I don't want suspicion falling on our farm. The children can manage until nightfall. Indeed, sometimes I wonder if we are even needed, they run the farm so well."

"A man's strength doesn't hurt in the fields. And they need our extra funds and protection."

"True." Arnost sighs then swings himself into the saddle of his roan mare. The horse huffs. "Come, Mikuláš. Let's find ourselves some gold."

It's a long ride to the road's narrowing, and the summer sun beats down on us as we trot along the track. We pass villages that are no more than tiny clusters of thatched huts surrounded by fields dotted with sheep. Soon enough, our path joins a rutted road populated by an occasional peddler or farm wagon.

23

When the main road to Rudná appears through the woods, Arnost slows.

"Let's circle around," he says. "Lie in wait at the rockfall."

I nod my agreement and follow the careful walk of his horse through sparse underbrush. A pile of gray rocks emerges through the trees. We leave the horses tied up to graze in a nearby grassy clearing, and Arnost leads me behind an outcrop. From here, we have an excellent view of the road.

A farmer with woven baskets of chickens in his wagon walks slowly by on his way to the market in Rudná. A messenger canters past soon after, his livery indicating his employer's stature, but we let him pass without harassment. We are after larger prey.

The sun is dipping toward the horizon when the jingling of harnesses catches my waning attention. I straighten and exchange a glance with Arnost, whose eyes are bright under his large hat. He nods and pulls a scarf over his lower face then quietly unsheathes his sword.

I adjust my own scarf and notch an arrow in my bowstring. When the carriage rattles into view, I peer at the livery of the driver.

"It's the carriage of Baron Veceslav," I hiss to Arnost. "This is it. On your signal."

Arnost nods, his eyes trained on the carriage. He raises his hand and waits. I pull my arrow taut.

He drops his hand.

I release my arrow. It flies true, straight into the driver's leg. The man yowls and drops the reins to clutch his injury. The horses whicker nervously, but Arnost waits for no one. He bursts from the outcrop and runs to the carriage, sword held high.

I follow, but my destination is the horses. They shy away at my approach, but I swiftly grab their strands and pour calming intention into them. They quiet immediately, and I turn to join Arnost.

Two guards have emerged from the carriage and swing their swords wildly at Arnost. The driver still moans with pain on his seat, so I ignore him and jump into the fray. My free hand is as busy as my sword, grabbing whatever lauvan I can reach. Within a minute, both guards are unconscious on the ground with only minor injuries. Before the past few years, I wouldn't have hesitated to dispatch these two, but the plague has brought so much death of late. I have no quarrel with them, and I don't have the stomach for senseless killing right now.

Arnost runs from the carriage, his eyes blazing in triumph. Shouts follow him from the elderly man and his young lady companion. He brandishes a small leather bag.

"Gold and jewelry," he says. "They gave me no trouble as soon as I showed them my sword. Come, let's leave."

With a few slices of my dagger, released from a sheath at my waist, the horses are freed from their constraints. In their docile state, they follow me easily, despite the hoarse cries of the driver. When we rejoin our own horses, I tie the newcomers to my saddle with spare rope I brought for this very outcome. Arnost leads us back the way we came.

When we reach a wide section of the road, I trot to his side. He turns shining eyes my way.

"It was a good haul, Mikulás." He jingles the money bag before slipping it inside his shirt for safekeeping. "This will keep the children fed for many months."

"We were lucky that the baron's carriage drove by. We could have been waiting a while for corrupt gentry to appear."

Arnost scoffs.

"They're all corrupt, save for our precious few allies that you have befriended. We can avoid those few, but the rest are easy prey. If we don't help the children, who will?"

CHAPTER IV

My restless dreams cause me to oversleep, but classes on Monday don't start until late in the morning, so I still have time to fill my fridge. In the grocery store, my hands full of chicken thighs and pork chops, a familiar face appears at the end of the aisle.

My heart sinks when she spots me and glares. Inna took the news of her friend Minnie's death badly—as did everyone who knew her—and, in her grief, she turned on me as the cause of her friend's demise. Her accusations were like spears in my chest—how could anyone believe that I could ever want Minnie to come to harm?— but I understood. The easiest thing to do in the face of senseless loss is to cast blame. Someone must be responsible. Someone must be at fault. Living in a universe that is so cruel is too hard to endure.

So, Inna blamed me. I didn't catch the full details as she railed at me on the front step of her house after I broke the news. I merely walked away, leaving her screaming obscenities at my back. Enough grief had pierced the fabric of my life. I didn't need the rantings of a woman in pain to heap more anguish on my sorrow.

It looks like time has not healed Inna's wounds. If anything, her eyes have grown more vehement in her dislike of me.

"You," she hisses as she abandons her shopping cart and stalks toward me. "You have the gall to wander around Vancouver freely, after what you did? At least have the decency to skip town so we don't have to see your sorry face."

"And what is it you think I have done?" My voice is calm, hiding the turmoil within. "Please, enlighten me."

"You know what you've done. Minnie died at the scene of a murderous cult, you monster. And you think I'll believe that it was a coincidence?" Her lips tighten, as if she has so many words to spit at me that she doesn't know which ones to choose first. "You met only a few months ago, and then you somehow convinced her to marry you right away. I tried to talk her out of it, but she was starry-eyed. What sort of Kool-Aid did you give her? Minnie wasn't like that. She was always methodical and thoughtful. Then her mood swings at the end—all the signs were there, and I missed them."

She turns away, blinking back tears. My gut twists. I'm sure it does look suspicious to Inna. Minnie and I got married soon after she touched the grail and released the memories of her past lives. It had seemed obvious to get married right away, since we were only continuing a much longer relationship.

The mood swings were from Minnie's emerging elemental side, which I struggled with as much as Inna did. But neither Minnie's past lives nor her mood swings were something she could have discussed with her friend.

Inna's self-reflection ends quickly, and she turns back to me with moist but hard eyes.

"You dragged her into it somehow, whatever was going on with that cult. You know what? I'm going to figure this out. You were involved somehow, and you're the reason Minnie's dead."

Inna's words cut through my fragile façade of calm.

"You honestly think I wanted Minnie to die?" I hiss as I thrust my face inches from hers. "I loved Minnie, more than you will ever comprehend. If there had been any real way to save her, I would have taken it."

Inna's eyes dart back and forth between my own.

"I think you're a really good actor," she says finally. "But you don't convince me. I'm going to expose you, Merry Lytton, for the fraud and murderer you are. Watch your back. I'm coming for you."

27

With those ominous words, Inna marches away, her cart abandoned at the end of the aisle. I stand frozen for a long moment. Other shoppers edge past me, unwilling to get roped into our whispered dispute.

Eventually, I shake myself out of my stupor and throw both packages of meat in my basket. I want to get out of this store as soon as I can. Inna's words rattled me more than I wish to admit, and I replay Minnie's last days again, searching for anything I could have done differently.

There was nothing I could have done, but the guilt gnaws at me anyway. I long for my next descent into the network to strip me of the emotions that plague me.

I take the long way home and pass Minnie's old apartment, where she lived when I met her. Our first kiss was on the doorstep of that building, and my eyes linger on the spot as I recreate the moment in my mind.

When a car honks behind me at my slow speed, I flash the driver a rude gesture and speed away. Minnie's office is near. She was a psychologist that I visited. It feels like long ago and yet only yesterday that she nodded at me from her comfortable chair across a low table. It took so long to recognize her true nature, and we had such a short time together in full knowledge. The thought still twists a knife in my heart a month after her death.

A strange smell filters through my helmet. Is something burning? I speed up and follow my nose to the source. When I turn a corner, flames lick at the blackened shell of a building. Firefighters spray water on the site, and the fire is almost under control, but my heart squeezes.

Minnie's office is gone.

The site of her passionate career is demolished, her legacy burned in a conflagration. My hands tighten on the handlebars until my fingers ache, and I stop at the side of the road before I cause an accident. How did this happen? It almost feels like a sign if I believed in signs, but I'm not certain what the message is. Is it telling me that she is irrevocably gone and all traces of her are being erased? Or should I conclude that the phoenix cannot rise without first burning?

I shake my head. A burning building is just that, nothing more. I stamp on my fanciful notions and swing my leg off the bike. The building is not Minnie. Minnie is gone, and she has no more cares for her former place of work.

But it's hard to shake off my regrets. I approach a spectator, determined to gather more information about the fire. She's a middle-aged woman with a crisp blouse over tailored trousers, perhaps on her way to work when the fire caught her attention.

"Excuse me," I say to her. She turns with a polite expression. "What happened here?"

"No official word yet," she says in a firm voice. This woman has a handle on every situation she encounters, I have no doubt. "But there are rumors of arson."

"What?" I'm dumbfounded. Minnie and her colleagues had no enemies. How could they be a victim of a deliberately set fire? "Why?"

"I don't know." She looks pensive. "It's a terrible shame. And in such a nice neighborhood. It won't help me sleep at night, that's for sure." She shudders then points toward an elderly woman speaking with a young couple on the sidewalk. "Talk to Gladys Freeman if you want more information. She knows everything that happens around here. Always peering through her lace curtains. Heart of gold, but there are no secrets from her."

I thank the woman and walk toward the other group. The young couple extract themselves from their conversation and hurry away. When the older woman catches my eye, I hail her.

"Ms. Freeman?" I say and close the gap between us. "A neighbor said you're well informed about the comings and goings here. What happened with this fire? I knew someone who worked in the building."

She doesn't catch my past tense, and her face grows concerned. She pats my forearm.

"Everyone got out in time, my dear. Don't worry about that. It's only the building that burned, thank goodness. Material goods can be replaced, but my Lord, what a mess to clean up! I wonder what the businesses will do in the meantime."

"The neighbor mentioned that the fire might not have been from a natural cause."

Gladys' eyes light up at the gossip.

"Quite right, quite right. I'm certain of it. Because who visited me the other day but a lanky young man with a proposition. He was knowledgeable about fires, and he offered to protect me from the spate of arson in the city. I hadn't heard of them yet, which as you can imagine surprised me, because I keep up with the news, but he made some good points. He offered to provide protection for a small fee." Gladys nods her head vigorously. "I've always been a believer in insurance, and I paid the fee. And I'm glad I did! Look what happened just down the road from my house. The arsonist can strike anywhere. An ounce of prevention is worth a pound of cure, so they say."

A neighbor cuts into our conversation, and I slide away. Gladys might be naïve, but I have lived too long to not recognize extortion when I hear about it. The "lanky young man" told Gladys, in effect, that he would burn down her house unless she paid. If she hadn't been so amenable to his honey method, I'm certain vinegar would have quickly emerged.

It's unfortunate to hear of someone taking advantage of an elderly woman, and I resolve to leave an anonymous tip at the police station. It's not my responsibility—I have enough elemental duties to keep me busy, I don't need human concerns as well—so I will leave it to the good folks in blue to handle.

An uneasy feeling creeps over me, and I frown and tune in more closely. Now that I think on it, the sensation didn't suddenly appear. I have been feeling it since I stepped off my bike, but enough commotion pushed the niggling sensation to the background of my mind.

I saunter to a tree in the sidewalk and lean against it as if observing the firefighting efforts, then my fingers grasp an earth lauvan that drifts upward on an unfelt draft from another world. I close my eyes and allow my conscious to descend into the earth network. What was a struggle a few months ago now comes as easily as breathing. My elemental side yearns to connect to earth strands whenever it can.

My inner eye opens to the world of lauvan and zeroes in on the issue. Flickering orange strands clearly indicate the location of the building fire, but underneath is a tangled ball of threads. Orange, blue, brown, and silver writhe together in a pulsing knot.

How did that happen? My conscious races forward and eases the tangles, but they are firmly lodged together, and the process is a slow one. Movement to my right catches my eye. Brown strands that snake from the tangle spasm and snarl together a short distance away. They must be reacting to the pressure of the knot. I feverishly loosen the tangles until every strand flows freely once more, then I release the knot in the earth strands nearby.

I come back to my body with a gasp. The first sense that returns to me is hearing, and panicked shouts reach my ears.

31

My eyes snap open and focus on the scene before me. Spectators of the fire now run from the site, and the man next to me babbles something about shifting ground.

I frown. The tangled earth lauvan must have shaken the road. No visible damage is evident, so the people gathered here must be startled, not hurt.

The fire is subsiding, and I nod with relief. Whatever happened in the network, I fixed it. The bigger question is, why were the lauvan unbalanced, and did the fire cause the tangle, or did the tangle cause the fire?

And who is this arsonist?

The excitement of the morning wears off, and I mumble my way through three classes and make the students read and discuss among themselves while I stare at the clock, waiting for the workday to be over. Not that being at home is any better, but every hour that passes brings me one hour closer to the weekend. I might plug into the network at lunch to check in. Yes, why not? I can't get much done in an hour, but I can at least speak with Tremor and Quake and monitor the lauvan. And the time will give me a reprieve from living in the human world.

Minutes after I arrive in my cramped office after morning classes, a knock startles me from my malaise. Wayne peeks his head around the doorframe.

"Morning, Merry," he says. His scarred face looks at me expectantly. "Ready for lunch? The deli brought in a new kind of sandwich. Curried chicken, I think. Worth a try."

"Not today, thanks," I say with a shake of my head. "I have some papers to mark. I shouldn't put them off."

I don't know why I'm lying to Wayne, except that I know marking will be a more palatable answer to my fellow instructor. He doesn't understand my fundamental duties. None of my friends truly do, and how could they? It's completely out of their frame of reference. They keep trying to tempt me away from my duties, so I have stopped mentioning them overtly.

"Oh, okay." Wayne looks downcast. "I was really hoping to get your opinion on something."

I almost waver at Wayne's slumped shoulders, but I hold firm. I need to check in, and I need a break from the relentlessness of human existence.

"Rain check. Let's try that chicken sandwich tomorrow, and I'll weigh in with my valuable and highly sought-after opinion."

I jog into the nearby forest with a blanket clutched against my side. Ever since I started my fundamental role, I have kept the blanket in my office for just such an occasion.

After deviating from the path for a few minutes, I spread my blanket on the damp forest floor and lie down. Quicker than thought, I close my eyes and descend into the network.

Instantly, the nagging ache in my chest subsides since I have no chest to feel. My mind is lighter than it has been since Sunday, and it's a massive relief. I don't want to forget Minnie, far from it, but I can't deny the ease of not lamenting her loss for a short while.

I drift around the network, not yet willing to search for irregularities in the earth lauvan quite yet. It's too pleasant to work. Now that I know they are there, elementals visibly drift among the threads of the world. To the untrained eye, they are almost indistinguishable from their elements. Water elementals swirl in waves at the shoreline, and air elementals swoop in silver puffs above. I send non-verbal greetings to fellow earth elementals as I pass, and they return my acknowledgement with reverence as they flow slowly in the ground.

I pass the site of this morning's fire at Minnie's old office building, and my curiosity sharpens. The arsonist is still at large. Is the culprit lighting a fire right now? Could I catch the strand-tangling as it happens?

It's a long shot, but I scout around Vancouver, searching for signs of fire. After three laps, I consider myself defeated. It doesn't matter. I have bigger responsibilities. It's time to examine the earth strands for signs of disorder. I send out a pulse of my intent and wait for sensations to arrive.

Tremor and Quake arrive first.

"Greetings, Earth," Tremor says. "We did not expect to see you today."

"I had a few minutes to check in," I say. "I can't be long. There's a snarl to the northeast causing melting permafrost, but I don't have time to fix it."

"I can take care of it," Tremor promises. "That's a task I can handle."

"I'll tag along if Tremor needs help," Quake says.

"Thank you both," I say. "You're my right hands."

The marking that I told Wayne I would do takes all afternoon, and I'm in a surly mood when I finish the last paper. As I shrug on my coat to leave, a knock at the door pauses me.

If it's Wayne again, how am I going to get rid of him?

Instead of Wayne, Alejandro and Liam wait in the hallway. I don't invite them in—I have had enough of sitting in my office for one day—so I step into the hall and close the door.

"Hola, Merlo," Alejandro says. "We're meeting Wayne for a drink. Will you join us?"

Part of me wants to say yes, but the larger part rebels at laughing and chatting right now. I don't have the energy to pretend to be happy, and no one wants a downer. None of them understands my current responsibilities, and I don't have the patience to defend myself and my actions. We are growing apart. It's inevitable, I suppose. It pains me, but it's also a relief. I can concentrate on my fundamental role without the distraction of human friends.

"Not today, thanks," I say. "There are some things I need to do at home tonight."

"I'll just have to ask you here, then," Liam says in a determined voice. "I was going to ease into it, but whatever. I've hardly seen you lately, so this will have to do." He glances at Alejandro, who nods his encouragement.

"What do you want to ask me?"

"Do you remember my brilliant idea to start a sword-fighting school?" Liam says eagerly.

I suppress a smile. Liam found out about his past lives— starting with Arthur-era Elian—and promptly joined Alejandro and Wayne in triggering as many memories as he could. Their favorite strategy was sparring with wooden swords I ordered for them, and Liam quickly grew so proficient that he wanted to start his own ancient martial arts classes.

"Are you still planning that?"

"He's past planning," Alejandro says with a proud look at his friend. "He's almost ready to open."

"It was a stroke of luck, getting that warehouse space off Cinder Street," Liam says. "And it will be very bare bones to start, but I wanted to get going right away. The more I teach, the quicker I will learn what people want and how to do it better. I already have some customers through word of mouth, but I want to line up a few guest teachers for when I start."

Liam and Alejandro both stare at me with expectant eyes. Their request finally makes sense.

"You want me to teach?"

I shift my satchel on my shoulder and yearn for the solitude of my apartment. More teaching is the last thing I want, but their puppy-dog eyes beseech me to consider Liam's request. What's the best way to extricate myself from this conversation?

"Fine," I say. "One or two guest appearances. Now, I need to go."

Liam beams.

"Perfect! We'll talk later when I know dates. Thanks, Merry."

Liam drags Alejandro away, but not before I catch his expression. It's a mix of pleasure at my agreement of Liam's request and also of frustration. I recall that Alejandro asked me yesterday to help him with his adventure dating service, and guilt twists my insides. I wave half-heartedly at my retreating friends and stomp toward the outside door. My life is too complicated for human friends right now.

The sun must be setting beyond a thick bank of clouds that weighs heavily on the sky, as the light is failing rapidly. I stride to my motorbike, but memories of the weekend plague me. I can't forget the destruction of that tiny Chilean town. Was it necessary? Tremor and Quake think so, but they are only regular elementals and don't have all the answers. I want the opinions of the other fundamentals.

It's time to call a conclave.

CHAPTER V

I pull on water strands to denude my saddle of rain droplets and throw my leg over the bike. Pacific Spirit Park is only minutes away, but I want to enter the network as quickly as possible. This day has been too long.

When I descend into the network from a horizontal position on my trusty blanket, I gather my strength. With all the intention I can muster, I release my summons in a massive pulse of energy that shoots away from my strands into the network and disappears.

My signature energy is distinctive and cannot be mistaken for anyone else's. With that signal, the other fundamentals will know I wish to meet with them. Because this is a pre-arranged signal, they will also know where.

With my message delivered, I direct my thoughts to the west. My strands follow, and I fly quickly past green and brown islands, then a vast expanse of heaving blue that represents the Pacific Ocean. Time is meaningless here, and eventually brown islands of threads emerge from the endless blue. I slow my pace and direct my path to the big island of Hawai'i. Soon enough, my destination appears as a flowing river of brown and orange strands that descends into tumultuous sapphire strands. Silver filaments dance above.

The site of our conclave is near Kīlauea mountain. There are other spots in the world that are similarly equipped to host the fundamentals of earth, water, air, and fire, but this site is the least ephemeral. Fire is a difficult element to predict, but here on this volcanic island of creeping lava flows, we have a somewhat steady source of fire strands. Being in our element is not strictly necessary—I can travel anywhere in the lauvan plane I wish—but it is more comfortable in the proximity of my element, and the other fundamentals feel the same. Until the volcano stops producing lava, this site will do nicely for a conclave.

Water is already there, as is Fire, both assuming humanoid forms for my benefit. I glide to a stop above a nest of brown strands which welcomes me with a sensation of familiarity and ease.

"Earth," Water says in greeting. "Welcome. Is all well in your element?"

"Mostly," I say. "But I have a question."

"Wait until Air arrives," Fire says.

We wait in silence, and I am lost in my thoughts as I decide how best to broach the subject. By the time Air whooshes in and assumes a humanoid torso and head within a silver cloud of strands, I am ready.

"Thank you for coming."

"We may be separate elements, but we are united in purpose," Air says. "Your concerns are our concerns, Earth."

"That is reassuring," I say. "I must admit, it's difficult to adjust to being one of a team. For centuries, I have been on my own. Being the fundamental has a steep learning curve, and not simply for the elemental duties, but having you three to rely on is a new but not unwelcome situation."

The other three send out pulses of agreement and comfort.

"But I am uneasy," I continue. "Yesterday, I released the pressure of an errant tectonic plate. The elements in charge had neglected their duties."

"Did you send them to dormancy?" Fire asks.

"No," I say slowly. "I gave them a stern warning, and they promised not to fail me again."

"You should take a firmer line with transgressors," Fire says with a sigh. "The lesser elementals must know their place."

"I'm sure Earth did what he thought was best," Water says. "We do not know the circumstances. Perhaps the elementals were sincere."

"I'll keep an eye on them," I promise, not wanting to get sidetracked by my leniency to the earth elementals. I still see myself in their ill-advised actions, but that explanation won't fly with the fundamentals, so I keep quiet on that front. "But that isn't what I hoped to speak with you about today. When I released the pressure on the plate, it triggered a strong earthquake that destroyed a town directly above. Many humans were hurt, and their dwellings demolished."

Silence reigns.

"And?" Air says. "What did you wish to ask us?"

My phantom eyebrows furrow.

"The needless loss of life," I say with exaggerated patience. "The wanton destruction. Was there anything I could have done to prevent it?"

The other fundamentals glance at each other with expressions of worry and condescension.

"It is not your concern," Water says gently. "You must keep the balance at all costs. I understand that it must be difficult for you, as a half-human yourself, but keep in mind the larger issues. If you hadn't released the pressure, imagine the consequences. Not only would the elemental plane be in utter chaos, but the physical world would suffer too. With earth out of balance, the other elements would be swept into a maelstrom of chaos, and fixing the resulting mess would be far more devastating than the original problem. For a physical world example, instead of one town destroyed, the whole region would suffer. Forests, animals, and humans alike would perish. The seas would rise in tsunamis that would wash over coastal regions, sweeping aside everything in their path. Wildfires would rage uncontrollably, ravaging vast swaths of land, and hurricanes would pummel the countryside. Do you understand now the importance of your role here? How crucial your prompt response to imbalance is?"

I nod my lauvan head. Water's words are logical. I can't deny any of them. A sense of unease still lingers, but I push it to the back of my mind. Water is right—I have a job to do, and it's an important one. I can't let my human squeamishness get in the way. If I don't fulfill my fundamental duties, what was Minnie's sacrifice for?

"I understand. Thank you for your words of wisdom."

We disperse after that, and I soar back to my body, filled with purpose that effectively squashes the remaining doubt in my mind. I have a job to do, and I will do it well. And the sooner I catch imbalances, the less destruction will occur.

When blue threads of ocean transform into browns of land, I slow and hover at Vancouver's edge. I might as well check for imbalances at home while I'm in the network.

I float over Vancouver's threads in a lazy search pattern. It was a long trip from Hawaii, and I'm both invigorated by being in the network and tired from the journey. Although it takes no physical effort, the outpouring of intention needed to transport me such a distance is wearing.

A few fires catch my eye as I travel, but they are all small things. Fireplaces or furnaces in houses, perhaps, or even clusters of candles. I wonder what the arsonist is doing tonight and when he or she will strike again.

I don't wonder for long. A bright blaze of orange flickers silently ahead. I race to the source and circle the conflagration. It's large and growing with the help of a flurry of silver air threads that whisk the fire into a frenzy of motion. The air threads move too quickly for me to sense any elementals within.

Below the flames, a knot of elemental strands forms, just like the fire at Minnie's office. I should untangle it, but a familiar cluster catches my eye. At the edge of the flames is a tightly woven cluster of human lauvan in three colors: silver of air, orange of fire, and peach of a human.

My half-elemental acquaintance Todd is here.

My strands race back to my body, and I sit up with a gasp on my damp blanket in the park. I haven't heard from Todd in months, ever since he was spooked by our first battle against Xenia and her elemental minions. What is he doing here? Either he is involved in the arson or is a key witness to the event. I need to speak with him, regardless.

I race to my bike and tear away from the curb toward Todd's location. Wailing fire engines direct me to the street, where red and blue flashing lights compete with an overwhelming orange glow. It's another fire, this time at a house in the same neighborhood as Minnie's office. The smoke smell is intense and acrid.

The house is toast, and the firefighters focus on saving neighboring houses and halting the spread. The house on the left shows no sign of catching fire, but firefighters work hard spraying the house on the right to extinguish sparks that land on the roof and singe the siding. This fire must have been more ferocious than the last.

Firefighters have the situation in hand—I hope—and it's more important for me to find Todd. I need answers, and I have

42

a sinking feeling he has them. I tuck myself against a garage and descend into the network with a thought.

The fire continues to flicker silently with orange lauvan, and the knot below writhes with painful-looking intensity. I must find Todd, but that knot needs untangling quickly. I scan the scene for Todd's telltale strands, and I leap toward my body when his distinctive cluster appears in a back alley behind the burning wreck.

Once my elemental strands are ensconced in my body once more, I run down the road and into the alley. Todd is almost hidden from sight behind a garage, but I know where he stands from my investigation in the network. I skid to a halt in front of him.

He starts in surprise and looks down at me from his considerable height. His brown hair is neatly trimmed, and his overcoat is stylish and expensive. He's a far cry from the rough-and-ready construction worker I first met months ago.

"Todd. What's going on? Did you see who the arsonist was?"

My words give him the benefit of the doubt, but I'm not surprised when his mouth quirks upward as if I said something funny.

"Merry. Of course you turned up. You're such a do-gooder."

I don't think anyone, in all the centuries I have lived, has ever accused me of being a do-gooder, but Todd has known me only for a short time. I admit, I have done my fair share of racing headlong into danger for others since his appearance in my life.

I shake my head, confused.

"It was you, wasn't it? The lauvan are messed up under the flames, so it didn't look natural. You started that fire with your abilities, didn't you?"

Todd shrugs and gazes at the fire with crossed arms and a nonchalant pose.

"I'm not admitting anything."

My ire rises. As a fundamental, it's my job to ensure that the elements remain balanced. The earthquake in Chile was a mistake made by ambitious elementals. But arson? This is Todd's deliberate plan.

"You're extorting money from the neighbors and burning houses of those who don't comply to sow fear in the rest. Really, Todd? You have the power of fire and air, and that's the best scheme you could come up with?"

"You're just jealous you didn't think of it first," he says with a hard look on his face. "Centuries, and the best you can come up with is teaching? What a waste."

I stare at Todd. Does he really think I haven't considered every angle of my abilities over the years? If I haven't done something, it's because it didn't sit right with me. Not for the first time, I wonder what Todd's upbringing was like under his volatile father who suppressed his son's burgeoning talents. It must have been a far cry from my mother's gentle protection.

"You can't do this. You're messing with the lauvan, and it's causing domino effects. The last building you burned caused a localized earth tremor." I draw myself up. "It's my job to stop you."

Todd spits on the ground then steps away.

"You can try, fundamental," he hisses. "But I've grown far beyond your lessons. Later, Merry."

Todd raises his hands, and a blast of air hits me in the face. I cover my eyes with my hands for protection then squint through my fingers and blink back tears.

Todd sprints away. I pull earth lauvan up, and the road beneath his feet shudders. Todd laughs, the sound drifting past his shoulder, and leaps into the air. With a whoosh of silver strands, Todd soars across rooftops into the dimness of late afternoon.

I reach for my own strands to transform into a falcon, but a rumbling turns my head. Shrieking follows.

A wide spilt in the earth runs between the burning shell and its untouched neighbor, growing wider every second. The tangle under this fire is creating an imbalance, and earth tremors are the result.

I can't chase after Todd, not if I want to fix this. I growl in frustration then plunge into the network once more. I don't know how long it takes until the last knot of the elemental lauvan is untangled, but eventually even earth and water strands that somehow twisted with the knot come undone. When I emerge with a gasp into my body once more, the concerned face of an older man stares at me through an unexpected deluge that pours over us. He grips my arm and shakes it.

"Sonny? Are you okay?"

"Fine, thanks," I gasp and look around for inspiration to explain my previous catatonic state. "The fire—flashback to an old trauma—I'm better now."

He pats my arm in comfort.

"You get yourself home, now," he says. "There's nothing more you can do here."

I need to stop Todd before he wrecks the balance any more than he already has. Each act of arson he commits makes the imbalance that much worse. How long before Vancouver is plagued by biblical disasters thanks to Todd's avarice?

The destruction of property and the human risk, while it

makes my stomach clench, is not my primary focus. I am Earth, a fundamental charged with maintaining the balance, and Todd poses a threat to that balance. He must be stopped, and it is my duty to stop him.

Fire and Air might be better suited to dealing with the effects of Todd's criminal ways, but I have the advantage of a body. I can stop Todd before he starts and nip this menace in the bud. I need to be proactive and use my abilities and position wisely.

Todd was born with powers and decided to use them for extortion and greed without considering the balance. Although he is of two worlds, he acts like neither a good elemental nor a good human. Minnie never trusted Todd, and the recollection hits me with a pang. She was right, as she always was. I wish I could talk to her about Todd now. She would have advice to give.

I shake my head to rid it of the notion. There is no point in pining for something that can never be. Who can give me advice since my dead wife is unavailable? Alejandro and my other friends spring to mind, but I dismiss them quickly. This is an elemental matter, and they wouldn't understand.

It's time for another conclave.

I trek back to my bike and wheel it slowly away from the smoldering ruin of a house. Not far away is a treed area next to a field and a playground. I'd prefer somewhere quieter, but this will do in a pinch. I find a quiet bench, reach to the ground, and grab the nearest earth strands.

I descend into the network and send out my signal. I feel like a child constantly requesting help from my minders but push the thought away. There is no shame in being new, and asking for help is better than fumbling along and making irrevocable mistakes. I can deal with Todd, but the *how* is what I want to confirm.

I finally reach Kīlauea, and the others arrive soon after.

"Earth," Fire says. "Another conclave, so soon? What troubles you?"

"The other half-elemental, Todd, is using his abilities to starts fires. I don't know why, but it's snarling the threads and creating imbalance. I will stop him, but I wanted to check with you about how to do so. He is skilled in manipulation of his elements, and I think his half-elemental status is giving him more power to mess with the balance."

Air frowns with strand eyebrows.

"Strange. Have your dealings caused imbalance throughout your life?"

"Not that I'm aware of," I say slowly. "Maybe fire and air are different? Or has he learned some new technique that I don't know?"

"In any event," Water says in a fluid voice. "He must be dealt with. I defer to your wisdom in this matter, Earth. Since you have a human body to work with, I imagine dealing with this miscreant in the physical world is easiest."

"As long as I have free rein," I say then shape my lauvan face into a frown. Seeing Todd again triggered questions I want answered. "Why was Todd born, anyway? And why is he the only half-elemental besides me?"

And Minnie, I want to say but can't. Her name doesn't cross my lips easily.

"That is a question we have pondered for some time," Fire answers with a flicker of interest. "Because you are the son of the previous earth fundamental, you have always been stronger than most. Indeed, that is why those closest to you are drawn to you again and again. Even after they should be properly assimilated into pure spirit, they instead retain a sense of themselves and join you in the physical world once more."

I take a moment to soak up the information. My friends

47

have been reborn again and again because of me. I suspected it, but here is the confirmation. That magnetism explains how I manage to meet them in every one of their lifetimes, despite the vastness of the world.

"Your strength has grown over the years," Air continues in a breathy voice. "Until even the barrier between the physical world and the elemental plane has thinned near you. Todd's elemental parents exploited that thinning and traveled to the physical world to create Todd."

"Why was it difficult for Xenia's minions to come through, if the barrier was thin?" I ask.

"They wouldn't have stood a chance if you hadn't been near," Water murmurs. "Your presence allowed the breach."

"Great, so it's my fault they came through."

"In a manner of speaking," Fire says. "But it's nothing you could have prevented."

"Oh, before you go, Earth," Water says. "There is one more thing. The half-elemental Minnie." Water paused. "My daughter who died. We were successful in petitioning for her immediate return. If she is not already in your world, she will be soon."

CHAPTER VI

My thread mouth drops open. If I could feel my heart, it would be pounding in shock. Without the emotional response of my body, my astonishment is more theoretical than physical, but Water's words still reverberate through my mind.

"Minnie's back?" I whisper. "How? When can I see her? Is she a newborn or an adult?"

"I believe she was or will be transferred into the body of a dying woman and then healed." Water looks apologetic. "I am sorry, I do not know where she is. Somewhere nearby, I believe. But do not concern yourself. She will be drawn to your presence, as she has been all your long life, and you will eventually find each other."

Eventually isn't soon enough, but there isn't anything else they can do. Already, their efforts are more than I had dreamed.

"Thank you," I say quietly. "Thank you."

My mind is in turmoil over Water's announcement during my journey back. When I enter my body once more, emotion slams into me. I gasp and shake with the news and my physical reaction to it.

Minnie. Minnie is out there, waiting for me to find her. Instead of decades of waiting with no guarantee that we would ever meet again, she is near. I bury my head in my knees and grip my hair with trembling hands. After the tranquility of the network, I don't know how to handle this outpouring of emotion.

I should check the lauvan before I go. A quick visit to settle my nerves will do the trick. I press my hands into brown threads once more and descend into the network.

Immediately, calm envelops me, and my mind quiets without the stimulation of my body. I set aside recent revelations and spread my senses into the network to search for disruptions.

To the east, a disturbance brews. I gather myself and flit toward the brown thread heights of the Rocky Mountains.

To my dismay, earth elementals are already handling the issue, and there is nothing for me to do. I float aimlessly for a while, then my body draws me back with an inexorable pull. The lure of Minnie, despite the strong emotions that come with thoughts of her, in undeniable.

I ride my motorbike home in a fog of questions, none of which have answers by the time I arrive at my apartment.

Walls are too constraining. I pace around my living room, unable to keep still. Minnie is back in this world, or at least will be soon. How can I sit in my lonesome apartment while there is a chance that she is walking in my city right now? If she is drawn to me, shouldn't I be out there, available to be drawn to? Hiding in my apartment will only prolong our reunion.

I have to leave. I dash into the bathroom and run a comb through my hair. My bedroom yields fresh clothes. I want our first meeting to give the new Minnie a good impression. My eye catches a wrapped bundle containing the grail, and I pull away protective lauvan to examine the ancient cup that swirls with multicolored strands. Its stemless bowl gleams with rust red and turquoise enamel patterns. Should I take it? It's the only way the new Minnie will know her true self. She will have to touch the artifact for her memories to pour back and my beautiful wife to return to me.

Although the grail isn't large, it's bulky for a pocket. But there are other ways to discover Minnie. Her lauvan, for one—they have always been an increasingly dark shade of blue—and shouldn't we have an immediate connection? Most of her previous incarnations triggered sparks between us upon meeting.

I nod with decision, drop the grail on my coffee table in the living room, and stride to the front door. I will hunt for likely candidates. If I find a woman who matches my criteria, I'll bring her back to touch the grail.

I can barely breathe through my tight chest at the thought of Minnie back in my life. I wonder what her personality will be like this time around. What will she look like? Her core will remain the same, I'm certain, but I'm eager to discover the new version of my darling wife.

The throaty growl of my motorbike punctures the evening darkness. I'm lucky we have a break from the rain—riding in a downpour is miserable, even if I can quickly dry off by pulling water threads off my pants—and the traffic isn't bad, so I'm downtown in minutes. I suffer a brief moment of panic—what if Minnie isn't downtown tonight?—but I dismiss the fear. I can only do the best I can. With any luck, the new Minnie will be drawn to me and I won't have to wander aimlessly for too many days.

I squeeze my bike in front of a parked red sedan and strike out for the row of restaurants and bars along Robson Street. Despite the darkness, or perhaps because of it, lights in the windows shine brightly, and rosy-cheeked pedestrians stroll happily in the dry night. Every woman that walks by, young or old, I scan for lauvan color. Twice, blue catches my eye, but when I turn with my heart in my throat, the shade is lighter than I expect Minnie's will be.

An elderly woman in an electric scooter trundles down the sidewalk toward me, and my heart leaps. Her navy-blue threads wave around her body in a loose cloud. I tighten my lips at her age—it would be a cruel joke if the fundamentals had placed my darling Minnie in a body that would count the remainder of her life in years, not decades—but I shake my

51

head to rid it of the thought. I don't care what body Minnie arrives in, only that she does. Of course, I would prefer younger, but I'm not fussy.

"Excuse me, my good lady," I say to the approaching woman with a winning smile. "Might I ask for directions to Granville Street?"

The woman turns her lined face toward me in surprise, then she uses every one of her wrinkles to transform her expression into the most impressive frown I've seen in years.

"Stay away, hooligan!" she shrieks in indignation. She lifts her purse out of a basket on the front of her scooter and tries to whack me with it. "I've got your number!"

I back off quickly and continue down the sidewalk to distance myself from the yodeling old woman. My heart pounds in relief. Minnie never reacted to me that way during any of our first meetings. I can safely strike the scooter woman from my list of potentials.

I duck into every restaurant that I pass and scan the customers for appropriately colored threads. Dark blue is a surprisingly rare color, and my search in each establishment is swift.

One pub I enter, a trendy establishment with atmospheric green lighting and a glass counter, contains a young woman alone at the bar. With a start, my eyes fasten on her gently waving blue lauvan. They are such a deep sapphire that they are almost black. Could I be so lucky?

I'm too eager for subtlety. I slide into the seat next to her and flash her a smile when she turns to me. She returns a less-than-impressed glance and purses her lips. When I open my mouth to speak, she holds up a finger.

"Don't bother with the pick-up line," she says in a nasally voice. "You're not my type." She looks me up and down and laughs.

My shoulders slump, but I examine her closely to make sure I shouldn't pursue further.

"Are you certain?" I say lightly. "I can be persuasive."

Another woman slides into the seat next to her and wraps her arm around the first woman's waist, who raises an eyebrow at me. I raise my hands, defeated.

"Have a nice night, ladies," I say as I leave.

I hope that wasn't Minnie. Although it would pain me to not be her lover, I could be content being her friend. However, there was no instant connection. If I can't find any other candidates, I might track down that woman and get her to touch the grail to be certain, but I owe it to myself to try longer.

After a few hours of searching, the restaurants empty, and my fragile hope is slowly crushed. When I pass a long line of shivering people dressed in sequins and tight pants, I slow my pace. There aren't many other places to search tonight except the clubs. I should check them out before I concede defeat for the night.

After a murmured conversation with the bouncer, and a few surreptitious pulls to his threads for compliance, I enter a hallway echoing with thumping bass and follow flashing lights at the end. A press of sweaty bodies gyrates on the dance floor, and servers weave between full tables.

I circle the room, searching for blue lauvan. A few women sport shades of blue, but none are dark enough for a new version of Minnie. After my tour of the room, my eyes scan the dancers, but my heart isn't in it. I have already written off this evening's search. Tomorrow I will try again, and again and again until I find her. Now that I know she is close, or will be soon, waiting is almost unbearable.

A flash of blue stops my breath. There. I walk quickly around the room to gain a better vantage of a woman surrounded by strands of the deepest midnight blue, so rich that

53

I'm astonished there are no stars in that velvet sky.

Her face is flushed, and a smile stretches across it as she shakes her hips with two other women. Her tight black dress glides over her curvy form in enviable closeness, and her straight brown hair leaves me breathless. It's almost the exact shade of Minnie's.

One of her friends is whisked away by a man and she latches onto him with drunken delight, leaving the other two to laugh and dance.

I was never a reserved man, and before I can think too hard about it, I approach the woman with the midnight-blue lauvan. It's too loud to bother speaking. Instead, I hold out my hand in invitation.

She looks down at it then into my eyes. A half-smile of interest plays on her mouth. Her friend elbows her in the side, and she laughs and steps forward.

I pull her close and we dance to the primal beat. My nose drifts past her hair and a familiar citrus scent nearly undoes me. This woman must use the same shampoo that Minnie does. Did. Used to.

I resist the urge to bury my face in her scented brown hair, although it's difficult. Instead, I soak in the sensation of her soft curves under my hands, painfully aware of how long it has been since I last touched Minnie.

When the song morphs into a new tune, I step back from her warm body with reluctance but mime a drink. She nods, and we make our way to the bar. With drinks finally in hand from a busy bartender, we maneuver to two empty chairs at the edge of the room. Here, I can finally make myself heard.

"I'm Fiona," she says quickly.

"Merry," I say. "Like the hobbit."

This earns me a peal of laughter that jiggles her ample chest in a becoming way. I grin back.

We chat about inconsequential things until our drinks are finished. With every word she speaks, every twist of her midnight-blue lauvan, every waft of her grapefruit-scented hair, I'm convinced that she is Minnie. I want this woman. I want to take her home, hand her the grail, have my Minnie come back to me. Could it be tonight? Could I be so lucky?

Fiona pulls me to my feet after she takes the last sip of her daiquiri.

"Come on," she says. "Show me more of your moves."

I'm happy to oblige, and we spend the next three songs pressed against each other on the crowded dance floor. I'm beside myself with painful hope. I need her number. I must see her again after tonight.

When she next pulls me to the edge of the floor, she presses her mouth near my ear. Her warm breath and the brush of her soft lips nearly undoes me.

"I'm not normally this kind of girl," she breathes into my ear. "But do you want to take me home?"

A groan escapes me, unheard in the pulsing beat of the music. My fingers clench around her waist. Yes, yes, a thousand times yes. Tonight, I might know. Tonight, my Minnie might be back with me.

"I hope you don't mind my motorbike," I say.

She pulls back with a devilish gleam in her eye.

"Sounds like fun."

At the bike, I hand her my helmet. This won't be the first time I've ridden without one, after all. Fiona straddles my bike and I kick it into action. She whoops with delight, her arms firmly around my waist. If I were a praying man, I would be fervent in my wishes that Minnie rides behind me.

The trip to my apartment stretches with suffocating slowness. When we arrive, Fiona minces through the underground parking in her heels with her arm tucked into mine.

"Don't look at me," she says with a chuckle. "This lighting is terrible."

I stop and place my hand on her cheek to guide her mouth to mine. What was meant to be a quick, affirming kiss deepens when she responds with passion. I slide my hand under her bottom as I press my mouth against hers, almost crushing her in my desire. I have missed Minnie so much.

She finally pulls away with a gasp.

"I hope you have somewhere more comfortable than a parking garage," she says with a breathless giggle.

"This way, my lady." I pull her toward the elevator, and she follows, unresisting.

We can't stop touching each other—small caresses here, a sneaky hand there—and by the time I close the door to my apartment, I'm worked up almost past endurance. The grail on my coffee table catches my eye. This could be it. Minnie could be back with me this very minute. I can barely breathe through my anticipation, and I pull Fiona to the couch. We collapse onto it, and her leg slides over mine. Her dress hikes up until lacy panties appear, and my breath catches.

"I would offer you a drink," I say in a hoarse voice. "But I have other things on my mind."

I swipe the grail off the table and hold it out to her, as if pretending to offer her a drink. She laughs and reaches for the cup. My stomach clenches. Her fingers wrap around the bowl, and I let go.

She doesn't react, and her threads remain steady. She examines the grail with curiosity.

"It looks really old," she says. "Like maybe I shouldn't drink from it." She chuckles and places it on the table once more. "Luckily, I'm not in the mood for a drink either."

For a moment, I'm frozen, then I lean back and close my

eyes as a wave of despair washes over me. I almost choke on the disappointment. I had convinced myself that Fiona was the one, that my Minnie had returned, that I could be so lucky as to find her today. The enormity of my search for new Minnie overwhelms me, and I can't move a muscle without fear of unraveling. The dashing of my desperate hope is too much to bear.

Fiona's leg slides further over me until her soft warmth straddles my lap. I still can't move, but she isn't deterred. Her hot lips kiss my neck, and the scent of her hair hits me in my vulnerable state. She smells like Minnie. My chest spasms with my hopeless longing for Minnie's embrace. With my eyes closed, the warm body on top of mine could be Minnie.

Fire scorches my body, heat flooding every part of me. My pent-up longing for Minnie is unslaked, even after the devastation of learning that Fiona is not her. I find Fiona's mouth, now darting small kisses against my chin, and push my own against hers, hungry for her taste. I squeeze my hands around her hips to rub her against me as hard as I can. She pants breathlessly and the foreign sound reminds me that she is not Minnie, but my body is too far gone to care. That citrus scent awoke a hunger and fierce longing that I can't control. I am undone.

I rip off her dress, her bra, but it's not fast enough. I groan with frustration and flip her around to force her on the couch below me. She squirms eagerly as I push my pants off and slide on top of her.

I'm rough with her, my burning need taking over, but she writhes with desire at the treatment. It only serves to enflame me more, despite the noises that are clearly not Minnie's. I desperately cover her mouth with kisses to block out the sound.

CHAPTER VII

When our lovemaking is done, we retire to the bedroom. After Fiona makes soft noises of slumber, I rise noiselessly, slip on my pants and shirt, and pad to the kitchen.

I can't sleep. My body aches for it after the release of sex, but my mind refuses to settle. I can't stop thinking of Minnie, and shame plagues my thoughts. It has only been a month and a half since Minnie died, and I'm already sleeping around? She would be the first to absolve me, I know, but I have to live with myself as well. Since I know she's coming back—and soon—guilt gnaws at me with relentless teeth.

I open the fridge and grab a case of beer. My patio beckons, despite the chill air, but I can't stay in this apartment with Fiona in the next room. I need space to distance myself from my shameful actions.

I tuck the beer under my arm, slip on my discarded shoes and coat at the front door, and exit my apartment. A bench is tucked around the corner from my patio, out of sight but close. It will do.

Darkness presses in, despite the orange glow of streetlights, and I sink onto the bench with a sigh. It's not until one bottle is drained and the next opened that I can think with composure on the evening. I searched for Minnie and was unsuccessful. I made a mistake bedding Fiona, but it was a mistake done in the throes of grief and frenzied longing. Now that I am prepared, I can avoid such a situation again. It may take a while, but I won't stop hunting for Minnie. All this pain will be forgotten once she is in my arms once more.

The second bottle goes down smoothly, and the third warms the chill of the night. By the fifth, lights appear in windows above me as people ready themselves for the day ahead.

I move to stand and return to my apartment, but I can't. Fiona is still in there, her soft body warm and welcoming, her citrus-scented hair too like Minnie's. I can't face her again, not like this.

My phone buzzes in my coat pocket, and I pull it out in surprise. It takes a few drunken stabs to answer the call.

"Jen?"

"Merry. Sorry it's so early, but I know you have class this morning, so I figured it was fine. I wanted to ask, will you join us for dinner after the grand opening of Liam's school?"

"Yes, yes, that's fine," I say, distracted. "Jen, could you swing by my place before work? I need your help with something."

"Of course." Her voice is warm, as if she is relieved that I am finally reaching out for help. "I'll be there in fifteen."

Fifteen minutes is definitely enough time for another beer. It's almost done when Jen's Prius zips into the visitor's parking lot. I wave at her, the motion making me sway alarmingly.

She jogs up with a concerned expression.

"What are you doing out here?"

"Drinking," I say with a grand gesture of my unoccupied arm.

"Yes, I can see that." She eyes my empty bottles on the ground. "I guess 'why' is the better question."

"There's a woman in my apartment. Can you make her leave?"

Jen stares at me for a long moment, then she sighs and sits on the edge of the bench next to me.

"Did you sleep with someone?" Jen tries hard to keep the judgement from her voice, but I know her well.

"The fundamentals said that Minnie was back, in an adult body, somewhere close. I was trying to find her. I got carried

59

away." I swirl the beer in my bottle. "Call me a fucking coward. It's true." My words come out surprisingly slurred, and I lift the bottle and gaze at the dregs of beer at the bottom with consideration. I lift my eyes to Jen's face, and my eyelids feel heavier than normal. "But I can't face her again. I can't see that hair, smell her scent. It's too much—too much like her."

I can't say Minnie's name again, but Jen's face clears with understanding. She nods and touches my arm in comfort.

"Got it. Leave her to me."

Before she stands, I catch a wicked grin on her face. It's unlike Jen but reminds me of Guinevere in her later years.

I toss back the last of my beer and listen for Fiona's exit. Muffled shouting turns sharp as the patio door opens. A pair of heels flies out of the door and Fiona stumbles after.

"Get out of my boyfriend's apartment!" Jen yells from the door. "Don't you dare come back. I'm watching his phone now!"

Fiona slips on her shoes and trots toward the bus stop. I lean against the bench, feeling guilty for kicking her out so unceremoniously. It's not her fault that I have unresolved issues and centuries of baggage. I hope she finds someone worthy of her.

I stumble to the patio door. Jen appears and waves me in then frowns at my less-than-stable walk.

"You're in rough shape," she says. "Don't you have work today?"

"Ugh." I sink onto the couch and put my feet on the coffee table. "Yes. I'll sober up soon enough. You'd be surprised how capable I can be while plastered."

"How are you getting there?"

Jen crosses her arms and raises her eyebrows. I shrug.

"Fly, I suppose. Operating heavy machinery while drunk probably isn't recommended in the modern era."

"Forget it," she says. "I'm driving you. Come on, get ready." She claps her hands. "Up!"

With a groan, I roll off the couch and stagger to my bedroom to dress. I may be distraught with Minnie's passing, but this time is eons better than any other. This time, my friends are still here.

But they don't understand my current life, and all I really want to do is descend into the lauvan network. My university job is nothing compared to my responsibilities as a fundamental, and the relief from my emotions in the network is an welcome respite. As soon as my alcohol-induced numbing wears off, I'm jumping in. It's time to check in, anyway.

Jen waits with a tapping foot at my front door while I change then ushers me to her car. My fingers work on my strands in the vehicle, and Jen glances at me before she pulls onto the road.

"Can you sober yourself up?" she asks.

"Unfortunately, no. I can mimic alertness and steadiness, but it's no true fix. My reaction time is still slow, and speech control is touch and go. Still, I'll take what I can get. My students likely won't tolerate another drunken class."

"Another?" Jen shakes her head. "Never mind, I won't ask. You're lucky my first meeting isn't until ten today." She drums her fingers on the steering wheel. "What happened last night? Tell me what the fundamentals said."

"Minnie is back, or will be soon, in an adult body." I wince when a strand tugs free of a knot at my temple. "The fundamentals managed it, somehow. She is supposed to be drawn to me—like all of you have been throughout the centuries—but who knows how long that will take? I went out to see if I could find her myself." I drop my fingers and sigh. "It was a fool's errand. I should have left well enough alone.

Then I saw Fiona, and I was so sure she was Minnie. Then she wasn't, but it was too late."

We are silent after my explanation. I close my eyes and try to ignore the headache building in my skull. I could fix it, but my hands feel too heavy to move.

"I'm sorry you were disappointed last night," Jen says quietly. "But keep in mind that Minnie is out there. You won't have to wait for long."

"Assuming I recognize her," I say with bitterness.

Jen turns left on Broadway and drives through a busy shopping district. Her fingers clench on the steering wheel.

"Look," she hisses. "It's Cecil."

I crack open my eyes and look out the window. Cecil, Jen's ex-boyfriend, formerly Lancelot in ages past, strides along the sidewalk with a grin and his phone held to his ear. He laughs, then puckers his lips to make a kissing sound into the phone before he hangs up.

We whisk past him, and Jen releases a long sigh.

"He looks happy," she says quietly. "I'm glad."

"New girlfriend already. I suppose my memory wipe did the trick. Now that he doesn't remember you or any of his former lives, he has moved on."

"Just like he wanted."

I glance at Jen, but she studiously keeps her eyes on the road.

"What was in that letter he gave to me for you to read after his memory-wipe?"

Jen is silent for so long that I fear she plans to ignore my question.

"He said he didn't want to be a third wheel," she says finally. "A second fiddle to Alejandro. He didn't want me to have to choose, like I always do. He said that this way, the three of us could finally be happy."

"And are you?"

Jen glances at me and smiles.

"Yes. Yes, I am. I wish Cecil could have kept his memories—I will miss him—but Alejandro and I are in a good place right now." She smiles, and her golden strands wiggle with true happiness. I suppress a grin of my own.

"You've given up on singledom? You spoke of being your own woman, choosing your own path, not letting the past influence you."

Jen makes a hiss of dismissal.

"Yes, yes, gloat away. You knew I would choose Alejandro eventually. So did I, if I'm being honest. I still wanted to feel like it was my choice, though, and that I really loved Alejandro and not just the others in his past." She plays with the steering wheel's rim. "But when he bought me my own practice sword, I think that's what made me realize everything I like about Alejandro, today."

"You're not a flowers and chocolate woman, I take it."

Jen elbows me.

"I like those too. No, it just showed me that he understands me, and that he wants me to be a part of his life as an equal, on my own terms. He's different than Arthur and the others, but also the same in the ways I like best." Jen sighs explosively. "This is all so complicated, isn't it? But I don't want to be complicated with anyone other than him. As for Cecil, I think I would have been fine if he'd kept his memories, but it would have been hard for him."

I nod but don't reply. Cecil may have couched his explanation to Jen with concern for her, but he confided in me that he wanted a clean break for himself, a life without pining for someone he couldn't have. Jen doesn't need to know that, though. She can preserve her selfless image of Cecil. He would have preferred it that way.

A sharp rapping on my door startles me the next day. It's followed by a muffled conversation.

"Come in," I call.

The door swings open, and I emerge from the kitchen, wiping my hands on a tea towel. Wayne appears, closely followed by Officer Kat Lee in plainclothes. I raise an eyebrow.

"To what do I owe the dubious pleasure of your visit?"

Kat Lee and I have an uneasy truce. She begrudgingly accepted my abilities the last time we spoke, and I left the battle at Xenia's temple before officials turned up.

Kat squints at me in suspicion.

"I have a few questions for you," she says. "Not in an official capacity."

"Oh, good. An unofficial interrogation." I wave toward the living room. "Make yourselves at home."

Wayne shrugs at me when Kat stalks to the couch.

"She wanted to talk," he whispers. "And I thought it wise to come along. I'm not sure what this is about."

"You and me both."

I lower myself into an armchair, and Wayne joins Kat on the couch. Kat drums her fingers on her knee.

"I'll get down to brass tacks," she says. "The department has received a tip that you were involved in the cult incident late last year, in an influential role. They've examined the tip and decided, based on lack of evidence, that it's not worth opening the case again. I saw your name and wanted to follow up." She leans forward, resting her forearms on her knees. Her sharp brown eyes gaze intently at me. "Tell me again about your connection to the cult. And leave out the magic mumbo-jumbo this time. You may have Wayne wrapped around your finger, but I'm not as gullible. I need solid facts."

My eyebrows rise. After a demonstration of my abilities a few months ago, she still doesn't believe me? It never ceases to amaze me how the human mind can dismiss cold facts and hard evidence as easily as a dream. Denial is a powerful force.

It's easy enough to prove my abilities to Kat—again—but I don't bother yet. I can indulge her questioning for now.

"The cult leader was the body of March Feynman possessed by an elemental spirit, but if that's too much for you to swallow, we can call her a madwoman named Xenia. Xenia had access to a large amount of money, and she used it to build herself a temple of worship. She styled herself the daughter of an Aztec earth goddess and convinced many hundreds of people to follow her and construct her temple. Again, I know that she used her elemental powers to coerce them, but you may call it brainwashing or charisma if it makes you feel better."

"This isn't news to me, but it's good to hear confirmation from you," Kat says. "What else? What's your connection?"

"Xenia wanted to recruit me, since I'm half-elemental myself. I refused but kept an eye on her. When she started gathering followers, I investigated, and a good friend was brainwashed. That's when it got personal." I allowed my mouth to twist in a mirthless grin. "From that point on, I devoted myself to stopping Xenia, but she was powerful beyond description. Eventually, our confrontations culminated in a pitched battle at the temple. I broke the coercion enchantment, but not before casualties occurred. And then—" I swallow and take a moment to master my emotions. "My wife died. In a rogue wave that swept over us and Xenia. Somehow, I survived, but Xenia and Minnie did not. They never found

65

Minnie's body."

In truth, I didn't let go of Minnie's body, but this is our cover story. I turned Minnie's body to ash and the air fundamental took her remains to the lake.

Kat stiffens at Minnie's name.

"Funny you should mention Minnie Dilleck," she says. "The anonymous tip said that you were responsible for her murder."

My body flushes hot with the accusation, but I maintain a calm façade.

"It was Inna Koslov, wasn't it? Your anonymous tip?"

"The informant's identity is confidential," she says, but the slight widening of her eyes tells me I'm right. She presses on. "Were you a member of this cult?"

"No."

"Your relationship with Minnie was a whirlwind romance, from our informant's report. Suspiciously quick, some would say."

"It was perfectly natural." Wayne comes to my defense. "They were clearly in love."

"Or maybe Minnie was hoodwinked and Merry here is an excellent actor."

My heart thunders in my chest, but I keep a straight face.

"So, what, you think I somehow brainwashed her into joining this cult—of which I was certainly not a member—which caused her death?"

"Maybe," she says, a hard glint in her eyes. "Or, you slipped her something to make her more malleable. There are options these days. Then you used her as a sacrifice for some cultish ritual that accidentally took out your leader."

My vision tunnels until I can only focus on Kat's intense face staring at mine. Blood pounds in my ears and all my senses are fuzzy. Is she seriously accusing me of murdering

Minnie as a sacrifice?

But Minnie was a sacrifice, in a way, and the accusation is too true to ignore. I can't maintain my control any longer, and I vent my guilt and anger at my nearest target.

"You have no right." I stand, my hands shaking with rage. Kat's eyes widen and she leans back into the couch. "You come into my house, under the hospitality of my roof, and accuse me of murdering my own wife?" I'm shouting now, unaware of anything except for Kat's frightened brown eyes. "She was everything to me! You have no idea who I am, what she and I have been through. You have no right. I would have moved mountains for that woman."

Kat's eyes flicker around the room, and it's only then that I notice movement. My lamp, papers to mark, dirty cutlery from the table that I haven't tidied away, all fly around me from the motion of my errant lauvan. In my emotional state, I lost control.

Hands clamp onto my forearms from behind, and Wayne's voice hisses in my ear.

"Keep it together, Merry. I don't want to pull you out of madness again."

I take a deep, shaking breath and willfully pull my strands back to my side. The lamp drops to the carpeted floor and papers flutter down. Wayne squeezes my arms once and lets go.

"Damn it," Kat mutters and passes a hand over her eyes. "I hoped that I'd made that stuff up. You really do have magic."

Her mouth twists on the last word, as if she can't bear to say it aloud.

"Yes," I say shortly. "I do. And Xenia was an elemental spirit. You are out of your depth here and dealing with things you don't understand. I suggest you keep this case closed."

"Oh, no," she says. Her fire is back, and she stands to meet

67

me eye to eye over the coffee table. While my antics frightened her initially, now anger burns. "You don't get to sweep things under the rug just because you have bonus powers. That's not how justice works. If Minnie Dilleck reached an untimely end, I'm honor-bound to find her killer." She narrows her eyes. "And if you are only half-human, as you claim, maybe that means your humanity is not as well-defined as the rest of us. Maybe killing Minnie wasn't a big deal to you, or maybe you even wanted to for some sadistic reason. How do I know what elementals are like? Xenia was a piece of work."

"Stop, Kat," Wayne says in a hard voice beside me. I'm glad he spoke, because I'm speechless at Kat's newest accusation that I'm a heartless unknown quantity. "Merry is as human as you and me, at least where it counts. His heart is in the right place, and he loved Minnie with a passion that you and I would be lucky to find in our lifetimes. There is no way he killed Minnie. Better to doubt if the sun will rise tomorrow than doubt that."

I breathe in deeply, grateful for Wayne's defense. I would take more comfort from it if Kat's accusation didn't hit so close to the truth. While I didn't kill Minnie, my involvement in the elemental world, my heritage, and the core of who I am played too great a role in her death. Minnie sacrificed herself because she was part of my life, and now I must live with that guilt and sorrow.

"Look," Kat says with a placating expression toward Wayne. "I believe you believe him, Wayne, but everyone is subject to trickery at times. Maybe Merry is a fantastic liar and a serial murderer, maybe not. I need to look at the facts, not my emotions."

My knees weaken with the weight of despair, and I sink into my chair once more. What does this argument serve? Minnie is dead.

"Do what you will," I say quietly and rub my forehead to ease the tension headache building there. "I lost the love of my life that day. I don't care what you think. I know the truth."

Kat is silent for a long moment. I finally glance up. She watches me with a curious expression.

"I'm trained to spot deception," she says finally. "And you seem genuine. Either you're an amazing liar or you're telling the truth."

I shrug. It doesn't matter what Kat thinks. The worst that could happen is that she will try to arrest me, and I'll have to skip town. It won't be the first time.

"He's genuine," Wayne says firmly.

"I'm not entirely convinced," Kat says. "But I'm willing to let it slide for the moment. I'll be watching you, though, so expect another visit if your name crops up at the station."

"Fine," I say in a toneless voice. "Are we done here?"

Kat nods and walks to the door. Wayne throws me an apologetic glance, which I wave off, and follows her.

"Wait." I stand. "Have you found anything about the spate of arson?"

Kat whirls around and pierces me with a look.

"I'm not allowed to discuss ongoing investigations. Why, do you know something?"

Her tone says she doesn't expect me to know anything, but her eyes search mine.

"Yes. I know who it is. His name is Todd Holland. But I doubt you'll find him. He's another half-elemental, and I'll bet he's good at hiding his tracks or at least escaping if you corner him."

Kat sighs explosively.

"Great. Just what I need, another magician running amok. What am I supposed to tell my superiors?"

"That's up to you."

"Can you find him?"

I stare at Kat. She looks both annoyed that she's asking me for help and hopeful that I can provide it. For a moment, I want to give into spite and ignore her request, but my desire to stop Todd overrules my ill will toward Kat. She's only trying to find justice in this world, which is an admirable goal, even if she pushes my buttons to get it.

"Sometimes," I say. "He's pretty good at hiding in the elemental way as well."

"If you get any leads, will you call me?"

It's my turn to sigh. I don't know what Kat thinks she can do, but maybe when she sees me acting for the benefit of others, I can sway her poor opinion of me. Not that I care what she thinks of me, but I dislike putting Wayne in the uncomfortable position of mediator.

"Fine. I'll call."

CHAPTER VIII
Dreaming

My arms are full of sticks and logs gathered from the nearby woods. Later, I'll take an ax and chop down a dead tree for firewood. Until then, this will suffice for cooking dinner.

I arrived a week ago to visit Nimue, despite the endless winter muck on the road rendering it impassable for a horse. My deer form has no such limitations, and since there is little for me to do at the villa, my heart led me directly to Nimue's door. Guinevere appreciates my company now that Arthur is gone, but staying in that hall without his presence is torture. The campaign season after his demise was brutal, and we barely fought off the hordes even with Framric's help. The winter rains were almost a relief, except that it gave me time to think without the threat of death greeting me every morning. Guinevere will have to make do with her maidservants. I have my own burden of grief to bear.

The other ladies have accepted my presence without much fuss. Arden regards me with calm acceptance, and Idelisa always has a smile for me, especially after I took over wood-gathering duties. They are currently training a new Lady of the Hearth, and the young girl from a nearby village travels to their abode twice a week for instruction. She is still too young to leave her family, and she scuttles away from me nervously when I walk by.

Her nerves don't bother me. There is only one Lady whose opinion I cherish.

When I drop my bundle by the door, Nimue approaches from the lakeside with a full bucket of water. After she passes the dead tree that leans away from the cottage, its hollow cavity black with shadow, she spies me. She smiles brightly, and my own mouth responds in kind. With swift steps, I close the distance between us.

She must sense my intention, because she carefully lowers her bucket before I lift her off her feet in a tight embrace. Her arms twine around my neck. Our lips meet, and I have never tasted anything sweeter than her. My kisses hold a touch of vital desperation, born of Arthur's death and the mortality of those I love. I wish I knew why I show no signs of aging.

When we finally part for air, she laughs breathlessly.

"You were only gone for firewood. Did you miss me that much?"

"Always." I nuzzle her neck, and she sighs in pleasure. "I don't know how I survive when I am away from you. I hate how we must live apart for much of the year. You are my wife, after all."

Nimue's hands curl in my hair.

"You cannot give up on—" She pauses, and I know she meant to say Arthur. My stomach clenches, but she recovers quickly. "On your fellow warriors and the people of the lowlands. They need you, else the land would be overrun with Saxons."

"And Angles," I say with a sigh. "The tide is rising, and I don't know how long we can keep the dam from breaking. I fear it is a hopeless proposition. And without—" I choke on Arthur's name, and Nimue strokes my neck. "Without a strong warlord at the helm, the other lords are dissolving into bickering among themselves."

"Can you not corral them into correct action?"

I laugh without mirth.

"I have always been an outsider to the Gwentish lords. They accept me, some even like me, but they would never gather under my banner, and not only because I don't have one." I

72

kiss her forehead. "Remember, I'm the bastard nephew of a goatherd from the northern mountains. My pedigree leaves something to be desired."

Nimue strokes my jaw.

"Still, if you don't fight and show them the way, who will?"

I sigh and hold her tight to my chest.

"Perhaps we should stay near this lake forever," I murmur into her hair. "Or flee to Eire."

The tromp of heavy feet reaches my ears, and Nimue stiffens in my arms.

"Who is that?" she hisses.

I draw away from her and reach for the ax which leans against the cottage wall. I would rather have my sword, but it lies beside Nimue's sleeping pallet. The visitor is likely a villager, but ruffians have accosted the ladies on occasion, and it pays to be wary.

Five men emerge from the woods dressed in the familiar robes of druids, and Nimue breathes a sign of relief before stepping forward.

"Welcome, honored guests," she says. "I am the Lady of the Lake. What brings you all the way from Eire?"

"Greetings, Lady," the frontmost man says. "We have come to visit with you, our fellows across the sea. It has been long since we have contacted those here who do the goddess' work."

Despite the winter chill, his robe is sleeveless to display blue tattoos that wrap from wrist to shoulder. I suppress a scoff—he clearly took off his cape for show before approaching Nimue's settlement—and glance at the other visitors. One in the back catches my attention, and I peer closer. If I'm not mistaken, it's Pert, an apprentice druid from my time in Eire. The gray in his hair doesn't entirely hide the faded auburn, and his beady eyes peer at me over thick jowls.

73

They widen in recognition.

"Merlin?" he says loudly. The leader turns toward Pert with a frown at his interruption, but Pert points to me. "That man trained at my side when I first joined the brotherhood. He ran away after releasing a sacrifice for the spirit ceremony."

All eyes fix on me. I hold my ground, although I am uncomfortable with the scrutiny.

"Surely, that was many years ago," I say, although their hard faces do not promise forgiveness. "In your eyes, I made a mistake, but I was young and foolish."

"You released a sacrifice who was expressly prepared for the goddess," the leader says slowly. "She does not forget, and she does not forgive. The hour may be late, but your punishment is due."

"What is this?" Nimue cries when they approach me. She stands in front of me, her slim young body straight with defiance. "There will be no harm come to my husband, and certainly not on my threshold. Stop!"

"We cannot, Lady," the leader says. "And, if you are indeed married to this abomination, you are contaminated also with his stain. Step aside before you mire yourself further."

"No!"

"Step back, Nimue." I heft the ax in preparation. "I have this."

The other men slide out swords with a chilling ring of iron. I swallow. Five against one aren't great odds, even for me, and the ax feels terribly inadequate. Thank the goddess for my other talents.

As if he can hear my thoughts, the leader pulls out a ring from a pouch at his waist and slips it on. It pulses with strands, and the energy it gives off is almost palpable from where I stand. I frown at the object, then my eyes widen.

My lauvan skitter away from the leader and wrap

74

themselves around my body tightly. What is that ring? I have never seen my own strands act like this.

I shake my head and strengthen my stance. The leader raises his hand and drives it toward me in a signal. With a shout, the other four run at me.

I disable the first man swiftly, and he crawls away with a bleeding thigh. The second man and Pert attack simultaneously, and I'm hard-pressed to defend myself. One sword nicks my stomach, and I gasp with the burning pain. My fingers reach toward Pert's strands, but he dodges in time.

My blood runs cold from fear, then hot with anger. I might not stand a chance, but I'm taking down as many of them as I can with me.

I swing my ax with a wild yell, and one man falls bleeding to the ground. I focus on the two sword-wielders in front of me and swing my ax again.

Everything pauses. My strands sizzle and spark, and I drop to my knees, unable to stand. The ax falls from my boneless fingers. What is happening to me?

The leader circles into view, his hand with the ring on the top of my head. His mouth twists with displeasure.

"Two of my men were grievously wounded by this stained abomination." He nods at the two swordsmen. "Tie him up and put him in that hollow tree."

Nimue runs forward, her face incensed, but Pert holds her back. She beats at him with furious fists, but he fends her off.

"What are you doing?" she screams at the leader. "Let him go."

"He disobeyed an order," the leader says calmly as the other man ties my wrists behind my back. "He disobeyed druids chosen by the goddess, and therefore deprived her of her rightful sacrifice. He will be left to starve in the hollow tree as punishment."

I'm in a daze and can barely move from whatever the ring is doing to me. I have never experienced something like this. The man tasked with tying my limbs with rope works unhindered. Nimue's face contorts in fury.

"No!" she screams. From a sheath on her calf, she pulls a dagger and stabs Pert in the stomach. He doubles over with a groan, and Nimue races forward.

"Get him in the tree," the leader hisses. "I'll deal with the girl."

I'm shoved unceremoniously into the crack that widens from the musty dankness of the hollow tree. With a growl, the man rolls a large stone over the entrance. It flops into place, sealing me inside the complete darkness of this earthen cell.

Cut off from the ring's influence, I am myself again. I strain against my bonds for a moment of panic, then I calm myself. It's only rope. I can escape such trivial bonds. Feverishly, my fingers pick at the rope's minimal lauvan, but it's a slow process. While I work, my ears strain to hear what transpires outside.

Nimue screams again, and my fingers grow frantic at the rope.

"Get him out!" she yells. "This is my home and my husband. Why did you come? Leave now!"

"We cannot leave this slight to the goddess unpunished," the leader says. "And we will stay to guard the tree until the abomination is dead. If you claim to serve the goddess, you will feed and shelter us until the task is done."

"Never!" Nimue shouts.

Footsteps pound on the soil outside. I struggle helplessly against the rope, my fingers picking apart strands with agonizing slowness. What is happening out there? Is Nimue in danger? I should be there with her.

A body falls to the ground. Footsteps pound. Another

76

scream from Nimue, then another thump.

Silence.

"Nimue!" I shout uselessly. I scrabble at my bonds, and finally they give way. With my shoulder, I heave at the rock. It barely shifts, but now that I have my abilities back, I can pull at the threads of the dead tree. The rotten wood at the base of the stone crumbles enough to loosen the rock. With another mighty push, I roll the obstacle out of my way.

I squeeze out of the hole on my hands and knees then stagger to my feet and survey the scene. Three men lie groaning on the ground, and another stares with unseeing eyes at the sky above. The leader's tattooed arms are drenched in his own blood, and he lies face down on the dirt.

My eyes see all this, but my mind only comprehends the smaller figure collapsed at the dead leader's back. I leap to Nimue's side, my heart in my throat, and skid to my knees at her side.

She groans, and my heart squeezes. If she's alive, hope is too.

"Nimue, love," I whisper. My fingers brush hair back from her face. I scan her body, and the terrible gash in her chest freezes my motion. No. No, this can't be true.

No.

My fingers race to untangle the knot above her wound, ignoring the wail in my mind that it's hopeless. This is too similar to Arthur's wound, and I couldn't save him. I can't lose her, too.

"Merlin," Nimue whispers. She coughs weakly, and blood dribbles from her lips. "Stop. Look at me."

My fingers keep working at their task, but I look into her clear gray eyes. She mouths a few words, her breath gone.

I love you.

My fingers stop. My body knows what's happening, even

77

if my mind rails against it. Without thought, I press my lips to her forehead. She closes her eyes. Her body gives one last shudder, then relaxes with its final motion.

My eyes burn, but the release of tears won't come. They build up inside me, aching for release. Cracks form in my mind, splinters of time and thought, fragments of Nimue and Arthur and could-have-beens and should-have-beens, pieces of who I was and who I can never be.

I can't stay here, there is nothing here for me. There is nothing anywhere, I don't even know who I am anymore.

I run.

CHAPTER IX

Despite my disquieting dreams, I wake up Thursday morning with fresh resolve to find Todd after my discussion with Kat. I have done plenty of questionable things in my past that I can take full credit for—I have no plans to record my ill-planned bank heist on Wayne's website—so it's especially grating to be accused of something that isn't true. My innocence here is worth defending, even if it's to a random acquaintance who doesn't really matter in the scheme of my life.

Still, Todd needs to be dealt with, and the police won't be much help. After my morning coffee, hastily gulped at the counter and chased by a dry bun from a few days ago, I march outside and find a quiet bench from which to enter the network. I could do it from my apartment, since it's on the ground floor and earth lauvan are easily accessible, but the connection is more robust when I can connect directly to the dirt below my feet.

I sink my hands into earth strands and close my eyes. Instantly, I melt into the network with relief. The constant squeezing of my heart that I'm almost used to is gone, along with elevated emotions left over from last night. I can view my argument with Kat dispassionately and set it aside as unimportant. Finding Todd and restoring the balance he willfully casts aside is the crucial point here. Everything else is irrelevant.

My strands float to the neighborhood of Todd's extortion dealings, and I'm both alarmed and unsurprised to encounter a raging fire with a tangle of elemental threads beneath it. After a quick survey of the area, I give up hope of finding Todd's distinctive triple lauvan cluster and dive into the tangle.

79

When I'm a quarter done, Tremor's familiar auburn strands approach.

"Greetings, Earth," she says. "I didn't expect to see you here."

"I'm dealing with Todd," I say with only half my attention on our conversation. The knot is a tricky one, and the fire above rages ever higher. Orange threads waver and flicker silently to great heights above my head. "He started another fire using his elemental abilities. It's messing with the balance, and I still don't know why. In the meantime, I need to untangle this."

Tremor watches me struggle with the knot. Although I gained instinctual knowledge and abilities during the transfer of power that made me the earth fundamental, untangling knots in this form is still new. I prefer fingers for this fiddly work.

"Can I help?" she says finally.

"I thought you'd never ask," I say with relief. "This is a sticky one."

Tremor dives in without further comment, and in short order we have unraveled the knot. Water threads in the surrounding area shiver at the release of pressure, then all is still.

All except for the fire overhead. I glance at it in consternation.

"Why is that still going?" I mutter.

"It will burn out in time," Tremor replies without concern. "It is the natural way of things."

"But people could be dying in that fire."

"It is not our place to meddle." Tremor's voice holds a hint of warning. "Remember your lessons. Our job is to restore and maintain the balance. I understand it is difficult for your human side to understand, but we cannot meddle in the natural order." She directs my attention to nearby water strands, which have finally stopped shivering. "If we hadn't fixed the knot—or worse, if we attempted to stop the fire—these water strands would react in unforeseen ways. Who knows what issues would arise for the humans if the knot had been left tangled? Although we left the fire burning, issues with water may have created a far worse problem, for them and for us. Don't forget about the greater issues at stake. Focus on the many, not the one."

My mind flashes back to the squirming pink strands of a trapped child in the Chilean earthquake, but I know Tremor is right. It's my responsibility to think of the greater good, not the individual. It's a difficult proposition for me, as I have only ever looked out for myself and a select few friends and lovers. But this is my task, and I will fulfill it to the best of my ability.

"Thanks for the help, Tremor. I'll see if I can find Todd in the physical world."

My gut twists with remorse as soon as I exit the network, but I ignore it and jog to the underground parking and my motorbike. It's time to find Todd again. Perhaps this time I can get the better of him. It's embarrassing that I have so many centuries of experience, and yet he can elude me. I thought I was better than that.

Traffic slows near the site, and cops wave us to detour around the burning house behind them. Firefighters spray water on the conflagration, but the two-story clapboard dwelling is a write-off. An ambulance waits on the other side of the street as two first responders load a man on a stretcher into the vehicle's open back doors. The man's exposed face and arms are covered in vicious burns, and my throat tightens.

"For the greater good," I murmur to myself when I drive past. Perhaps if I repeat it often enough, I will believe it.

I circle the neighborhood in my search for Todd, but my heart knows he's long gone. When my phone vibrates in my pocket, I pull over and slide it out with a sigh of dejection.

It's a text from Alejandro, asking me to swing by Liam's new studio. I don't have anything better to do right now, since I don't have class for another hour, so I turn my wheels to the eastern end of downtown where Liam found a warehouse room to rent cheaply.

I park my motorbike in the loading zone out front and knock sharply on the door of the address Alejandro sent. Large glass windows are covered with newspapers to hide the transformation inside, and I find myself idly reading classifieds until the door clicks open.

"Good, you got my text." Alejandro is dressed in a paint-smeared shirt and his thick hair is even more unruly than usual. "Come in."

The smell of fresh paint hits me as I enter, and I blink at bright track lighting suspended from the tall ceiling. Liam is on the far side of the space, red-faced and panting, but he waves at my entrance. Cream-colored walls gleam with wetness in patches, and a stack of tall mirrors waits to be hung at the back. Alejandro beams at me.

"What do you think?"

I nod and look around.

"It's an upgrade from the dung-scented courtyard I taught you in."

Alejandro laughs. Whether Alejandro or Arthur, he always extracts my lighthearted side.

"Modern folk don't know how lucky they have it. Hold on, let me put this down."

He walks to a folding table and places a stack of papers onto it. I peer at the forms.

"What's all this?"

"Liam has paying classes starting next week, but he managed to scrape up some sponsorship money to offer a class to underprivileged youth. I'm processing application forms for him."

"Don't you have work today?"

"Soon. I'm almost done here, then I'll go. Anyway, this is important. I have to prioritize my efforts to match what I believe in. My job matters, but this matters more. At the end of this life, I want to be proud of my choices. I'll find a way to make things work, no matter what happens."

I shake my head, but not in denial of Alejandro's values. I admire him, although I expect I would value that which brought in money to pay for my necessities more than filling out forms. I suppose his values are even more important to Alejandro now that he might remember this life far into the future.

"Well, it looks good in here. Is this where I'll be holding my guest classes?"

"Yes. Grand opening is tonight. As soon as Liam finalizes the dates, he'll let you know. I think he wanted you early in the session."

I watch Liam rolling out a practice mat, grunting with effort, but I don't see him. Instead, my mind curdles around the burned man in the ambulance and what I could have done differently. I'm no stranger to death—indeed, I have caused my fair share in battles and duels—but there's something different about ending someone's life while they relax at home, unaware. One moment, the man was eating toast and listening to the news, and the next he is a piece of toast on the news. That was me. Me and Todd, of course, I won't forget to give Todd plenty of credit. But I was there, and I had the power to stop the burning.

I know it's my duty to uphold the balance above everything, but I can't let it go.

"What's up, Merlo?" Alejandro looks curiously at me. "You look like you ate something funny."

"When I'm the fundamental, I must do things to keep the balance for the good of the world." I'm not sure why I'm telling Alejandro this—I haven't wanted to share my fundamental life with my friends because they wouldn't understand—but I can't stop my mouth from blurting the words out. "But there are sometimes human consequences. And I can't help them without neglecting my greater role as balance enforcer."

Alejandro gazes thoughtfully at Liam, who is now heaving a second mat into place.

"Keeping the balance is the right thing," he says finally. My gut relaxes at Alejandro's approval but clenches again at his next words. "But what is the point of doing the right thing if you lose your humanity along the way?"

Alejandro turns to me, and I flick my eyes away from his earnest expression.

"Look at me, Merlo," he continues. My eyes travel unwillingly to his face. "You've been hiding from us ever since the battle against Xenia. Jen insists that you're mourning Minnie, and for a while I let it slide. But it's not that, is it? This fundamental role is changing you."

My jaw tightens. Alejandro hasn't lost the insight into others that made Arthur a great leader.

"If you want to live in the world," he continues. "You need to take part in it. You can be both human and fundamental. Don't forget your human side. You need it. Minnie would want you to keep it. Don't throw it away by giving up on your humanity."

My lips tighten. Alejandro's words only serve to remind me why I haven't confided in him before. He doesn't understand the paramount importance of the balance. How could he? He is unequivocally human. I have the misfortune of seeing both sides of the coin, and Alejandro's black and white are a murky gray to me.

There's no point in explaining this to Alejandro. I know his opinion will be firm. Instead, I change the topic.

"What was in the letter Cecil gave you?" I ask. "Before I wiped his memory?"

Alejandro's strands squirm.

"He told me he had no ill will toward me," he says after a pause. "And that he wished Jen and I would be happy together. I felt like a jerk after, to be honest, and then I couldn't say anything back, because you'd already wiped his mind. Was that really what he wanted?"

I shrug.

"He was adamant. He looked content when I passed him on the street a few days ago. And, who knows, perhaps you'll see him in another life, and you can say your piece then." I check my watch. "I should get moving. Class starts shortly, and I don't want to get probation again. I'm already skirting the line as it is."

Alejandro nods, but the set of his mouth tells me he's disappointed in our truncated conversation. I ignored his advice and retreated from discussing it. I raise my hand to Liam and swiftly depart, but I can't help wondering how much strain our friendship can take.

Perhaps it's for the better. Without others to tie me to my human life, I can devote myself to the elemental realm. With greater exposure to the elementals, perhaps my qualms about the consequences of my duties will fade.

I slouch through the hallway at work after my first lecture. I have an hour to mark papers before my next class.

I could mark papers, but it's more likely that I'll grab a coffee and stare at the wall, wishing this day over so I can enter the network. The world feels very heavy today, and slipping into lauvan will allow me to shed that weight.

"Merry," a female voice calls out.

I stop and turn. The dean strides toward me, and milling students part to clear a path. I sigh and think regretfully of the coffee that will have to wait.

"Good morning," I say.

"Merry, how are you?"

The dean's concerned expression might have undone me a week ago. Today, I don't have the energy to care about anything except the dull ache that pushes me to enter the network.

I'm not fine, and I have no reason to lie to please her. I have no problem lying, but only if it benefits me. Making the dean feel less uncomfortable matters nothing to me. But saying that the only thing keeping me going are visits to an ethereal plane of existence would not spark confidence in my abilities as an employee, so I'll keep that under wraps.

"I'm managing."

The dean's look of concern deepens, and she pats my arm.

"Of course. It's a difficult time. If there's anything I can do, don't hesitate. And please take advantage of counseling services that the university provides."

My face twitches at the memory of Minnie, my first and last therapist. The dean misconstrues my expression.

"There is no shame in reaching out for help," she says

sternly. "Please remember that."

I nod because it's what she expects, and she nods back in satisfaction.

"I'm pleased with how well your classes are progressing after your probation," she says quietly so passing students won't overhear. "Especially given your recent misfortunes, you have exceled. Thank you for being a valuable member of this department."

I nod again, wishing she would stop talking and leave me alone. I want to be by myself with my hot beverage, but I don't have the energy to finish this conversation on my own. A vision of my bed pops into my mind, and I ponder the appeal of sinking into a sleepy melancholy like I usually do after a death. If I didn't have the retreat of the network, I would crawl back to bed right now.

The dean pats my arm again.

"I'm glad to hear you're doing all right. Just knock on my door if you need anything."

With a nod of a job well done, she sails off. I sigh in relief and direct my steps to the coffee kiosk.

After my final class, I roar to Pacific Spirit Park and pull my bike to the side of the road. A few minutes of walking brings me to a quiet dell, and I spread my blanket for a quick dip in the network. I can't wait until the weekend to feel the relief of the elemental plane. In any event, there might be issues that need resolving.

My elemental lauvan slip into the network with the ease of cutting butter, and the relief is palpable. No longer does my body feel like it is being squeezed from the pressures of grief and responsibility. Instead, I am weightless, objective, and ready to tackle my tasks. It is freeing.

I float around Vancouver without direction simply to revel in the feeling of being without physical sensations. There are so many lauvan clusters of every hue from all the living things crammed into a city. Heaving blue threads surround us from the sea, and brown strands lie still and calm like a carpet under everything.

I don't know how long I spend aimlessly scanning the view, but when familiar strands wink into existence, I rush closer for a better look. Todd's three-color cluster, orange and silver and peach, blinks out of sight before I approach, but I know it's him.

My strands hover on the spot in my astonishment. Todd was there, I know it. But how did he disappear? Xenia and her minions disguised themselves so they couldn't be found, but I don't know their secret. How did Todd figure it out? I resolve to ask the other fundamentals the next time I see them. That is a trick I want up my sleeve.

However he hid his location from elemental sight, one thing is clear. Only people doing suspicious things tend to hide their actions. Is Todd starting another fire? Perhaps this is my opportunity to catch him in the act. And this time, I'll take him down.

I flow back to my body and sit with a gasp. The sun must be setting somewhere high above the heavy gray clouds because the light is dim. I leap up, roll my blanket into a loose pile, and jog to my bike in the hopes that some exercise will stop the shivers that rack my body. The weather is too cold to lie on the forest floor, but the sacrifice is worth the weightlessness of the other plane.

My foot hits the kickstand and I swerve into traffic ahead of an irate pick-up. I can't miss Todd again, so I pass the next vehicle and take a hard left. I gun the bike and make it to Todd's chosen neighborhood in record time.

No fire trucks wail, and the smell of burning wood is absent. Perhaps I was mistaken. Todd might be in the neighborhood, but he hasn't yet started a fire.

Still, I want to find him. He might be innocent today, but his track record is stained with past transgressions. If I can find him and stop the imbalances he's creating, my job as fundamental will be far easier.

I slide my bike into a tiny gap between parked cars—they might not be able to leave, but technically there is room for me—and continue on foot. Without Todd's visible lauvan signature in the other plane, my search is relegated to the physical world. There are many streets in this neighborhood, not to mention alleys, gardens, and garages to hide among. I break into a jog to cover more ground.

Ten minutes of searching passes with no sign of my quarry. I stop in the middle of an alley, breathless and sweaty, and kick a loose stone at a nearby garage door in my frustration. I hate being two steps behind. I'd much rather be the one running than the chaser. I have more experience at evading capture.

An acrid smell wafts past my nose, and I sniff. Burning tar from an asphalt shingle roof, if I'm not mistaken. Todd has struck again.

I don't know where the fire is, and the quickest way to find out is in the network. My fingers grasp the nearest earth strands at my feet, and I plunge into the other plane. Only a block away, gouts of fire flicker up the side of a tall structure, and a telltale tangle of elemental strands is clustered underneath.

Todd is nowhere to be seen, and I curse my luck. If I don't untangle the knot now, the consequences could be dire. It's my job to think of the balance first, even before my manhunt. Perhaps I can resolve the issue quickly enough to search for

Todd once more.

I work as swiftly as I can, but unknotting lauvan is tedious work. When I unravel the last knot, a shiver of air threads passes overhead. I wince at the reminder of the imbalance I avoided.

Once I'm back in my body, sound is the first sense to return. A cacophony of noise hits me: shrieking sirens, shouting, sloshing water, screaming. I shake off the overwhelm of physical sensation and run toward the noise. The smell is worse now, and mixed with tar and wood is the unmistakable scent of burning flesh. I pick up my pace.

Around the corner, the fire is obvious. A small bungalow is a burning torch now, and no volume of water will save it. I race to a small group of spectators huddled on the far side of the road from the fire trucks and skid to a halt.

"What happened?" I gasp. A young woman with tear-streaked cheeks turns to me.

"The arsonist struck again," she says with a hiccup. "But this time, a freak wind blew through and pushed flames toward the neighbor's yard. Ben didn't have time to move, or shout, or anything. He just lit on fire and…" She covers her mouth with a hand. Her horrified eyes stare into mine, begging me to stop making her describe the event.

My jaw clenches. I have no need to hear further details. The unfortunate Ben didn't stand a chance. I might have prevented some unknown future catastrophe, but that's not much consolation to Ben's family.

There must be something I can do. Now that the knot is untangled, surely I can calm the fire, just enough for the firefighters to get a handle on the situation. I walk away from the group and lean against a tree on the boulevard.

But when I slip into the network again, Tremor is waiting for me.

"I wondered if you would come back," she said. "I'm here to remind you of your duties."

"I untangled the knot," I say. What is she getting at? "What else do I need to do?"

"It's what you need to not do." She circles the flickering orange strands of the house fire. "You can't help, Earth. You must let the natural world take its course."

"It's not natural," I snap. "Todd lit this fire."

"It started as an elemental problem," she says calmly. "But you resolved that, and now it is natural. Trying to stop the fire would only upset the balance, especially if accomplished by you. Never forget how much power you wield. A tweak from you echoes throughout the plane."

My strands curl into a ball against the logic of Tremor's words.

"I have to let the firefighters put the fire out?"

"Yes, you do."

I flow back to my body without another word. Tremor might be right, but it doesn't mean I have to like it. Predictably, my gut clenches with guilt and shame once I land in my body, but a click distracts me from my emotions.

Officer Kat Lee closes the second handcuff around my wrist with a grim expression.

"Merry Lytton, you're under arrest," she says loudly for the benefit of her partner, who stands a few paces away. More quietly, she says, "I know you insist you're innocent, but you're at the scene of a crime without first calling me about Todd Holland's whereabouts. I have enough suspicious behavior to bring you in without even mentioning the magic stuff. If you're the one behind these fires, you'll pay for your crimes."

CHAPTER X

Kat Lee thinks she has me, but I've never been one for captivity.

I release a wordless shout. When Kat jumps in surprise, I wrench my hands out of her grasp with a swift jerk upward. She twists off balance with the motion, and I dart away with a speed born of desperation and long practice. Shouts erupt behind me, but I hurdle over a low fence and into a tiny backyard that connects to the alley.

While I run, my fingers fumble with the strands of the handcuffs. They don't have many, but enough filaments wrap around the locks from the handcuff's height that it's a matter of seconds before the cuffs click open. I let them fall onto the alley's crumbling pavement. Mindful of approaching shouts, I yank at my lauvan and transform into a bird.

My wings labor to carry me away, but not before I catch sight of Kat's slack-jawed mouth. Her partner scans the alley, unaware that his target soars far above him. I'm tempted to show them my appreciation with a well-aimed bird bomb, but I resist with the utmost restraint and aim my wings toward home.

My heart sits heavily in my feathered chest, and I ponder my situation in the relative peace of flight. I am often run out of town when others discover my secrets, but I hoped that I could stay in Vancouver for longer than this. I might be wondering about my place in the world, but to be uprooted so unceremoniously rankles. I like to be the one making the choices.

Perhaps this is an opportunity disguised as a tragedy. I am changing—even Alejandro has noticed—and I am not who I once was. My friends and I are growing apart, and perhaps I need to make a clean break. A quick vanishing would hurt initially, but then they could move on without my mournful presence in their lives.

I can go anywhere, and Minnie will eventually be drawn to me. My wings flap harder in my determination. Yes, it is time to make a silk purse out of this sow's ear.

I fly in a direct line to my apartment, much faster than a police cruiser can drive despite the heaviness in my wings from my lack of earth connection. I will have a few minutes to collect my things. I circle to the lawn and transform before I hit the ground so my transition from flight to walking is seamless.

Once in my apartment, I scan my possessions. The ones I truly care about are few indeed. The grail is my priority—without it, Minnie is forever lost to me—so I scoop it out of my closet first and into my coat pocket. Into my satchel goes my sketchbook filled with images of Minnie and my friends throughout the ages. Other than those items, what do I care about? A few knickknacks from my travels adorn my bookshelf, and my harp leans against the wall. I have no passion for music, not since Minnie died. If she returns to me and I discover joy again, I will find another instrument.

I tuck some bread and cheese into my satchel, along with spare underwear and my toiletries, then I'm ready. My eyes rake over the small apartment, which is devoid of pictures or any real sense of personality. I never saw the point, especially after Minnie. Now, I congratulate myself for my foresight. It's much easier to leave when I'm not leaving anything behind.

I close the door to my apartment and the latch clicks with a finality that makes my muscles tense. Another life gone, another new beginning starts. The thought brings me no joy, and I contemplate the vast expanse of my future life with a sinking heart. I hope Minnie comes back to me. I hope she can find me when I'm on the run. I don't want to do this alone.

But perhaps I need to. My fundamental duties and my human life grow more incompatible with every passing day. I can't make the decisions I need to make while still clinging to my humanity. Would Minnie fit into this new life? Worse still, what if I find her, wake her memories from their slumber, and then she must endure the half-life which is the only one I can give her? Would it be better to let her live her life unencumbered by my fundamental nature? If I truly love her, can I let her be?

Not likely. I'm too selfish for that. But the notion does give me pause and introduce disquiet to my plans.

I'll have to cross that bridge when I come to it.

Sirens wail in the distance, and I thunder down the stairs to the parking garage and run to my motorbike. The sirens are for me, I have no doubt, and I need to get away before they reach me.

A few twists of my motorbike's sparse strands, and it morphs from black to electric blue. The license plate's numbers wriggle until they spell "SHW OFF", then I turn to my own strands. After a moment's fiddling, my features meld into a new shape. In the left rearview mirror, a shaggy blond head with piercing blue eyes stares at me with a hard expression. It will do.

I shove my helmet on my head and kick the bike on. It roars with approval, and I peel out of the garage with a squeal of tires. On the road, I pass the visitor's parking lot where two police cruisers slam to a stop. Officers leap out of their doors. My mouth twists in grim satisfaction at my narrow escape, and I gun it down the road.

It isn't until I pass the next intersection that I realize I don't know where I'm going. Now that I'm on the run, the sensible course of action is to skip town and start somewhere new. The thought brings me no pleasure, but even less when I consider Todd. He's a yet-unresolved problem, and he's mine to solve. Alone among the fundamentals, I am uniquely positioned to stop him, especially since he has figured out how to hide his strands from detection in the elemental plane. I can't leave him to create disturbances in the network.

My heart pounds from adrenaline and frustration, and I want nothing more than to be immersed in the network to relieve myself of the burden of human emotion. It's exhausting, especially now that I know how freeing it is to be without. I can ask the fundamentals about Todd's hiding ability while I'm there.

I take a sharp right ahead and turn into Queen Elizabeth Park. It's a sprawling collection of lawns, gardens, playing courts, and trees draped over a hill in the center of Vancouver. I drive around the circle and pull over. A cedar tree beckons, its branches thick enough that the ground underneath is still dry even after recent rains. I lope toward it and settle myself against the trunk.

A quick text to Kat Lee is my first order of business. I doubt she'll believe me after today, but reminding her of our true adversary is the only thing I can do. She is a diligent police officer who will follow any leads she is given.

I'm not your enemy. Watch Todd Holland to find your answers.

Once my message sends, I tuck my phone in my coat pocket, pull a protective shield of earth strands over me, and enter the network.

As a matter of rote, I quickly scan Vancouver for signs of Todd's tripartite strands but find nothing. Disappointed but not surprised, I splinter my conscious into hundreds of parts and send them searching for the nearest fundamental. I could call another conclave, but my question doesn't need the expertise of all fundamentals. Besides, I keep calling conclaves, and I hate feeling like a whining child asking his elders for help. It bruises my dignity.

Fire is the closest, busy at an active hot spot under Yellowstone National Park. At the prodding of my conscious, the fundamental flows toward me. Where earth and fire meet in molten magma at a deep point of the hot spot, we join to converse.

"Earth," Fire greets me. The fundamental's strands blast me with their distinctive brand of surging furnaces and crackling wildfires. "Greetings."

"Fire." I don't waste time with niceties. Elementals don't usually bother with them, and I have more pressing matters. "Todd, the half-elemental I'm pursuing, has figured out how to mask his threads. Now, I can't find him in the network. Is there a way to uncover him? Also, how is it done? I feel wrong-footed not knowing this trick."

"Hiding your lauvan is a higher-order elemental ability, taught to lower elementals when they achieve a higher level," Fire replies. "We discourage it, as it makes keeping tabs on lesser elementals difficult, but there isn't much we can do about it."

"Todd must have been taught by another elemental. I wonder who." I shake my strand form's head to indicate the thought isn't important. "So, you can't undo it?"

"Unfortunately, no. You will have to search for him in the physical world. As for learning the technique yourself, it is quite simple if you have enough power, which isn't a problem for you. Twist one of your strands like this and concentrate on concealing yourself."

I follow Fire's directions, and my strands fade until they are insubstantial wisps.

"Avoid staying in that state unless you must," Fire says.

"We fundamentals cannot find you in that form."

"Noted." I untwist my strands, and my chocolate brown lauvan reappear. "I like knowing that Todd can't find me if I don't want him to. Now, I only have to find Todd in a city of almost three million people. Piece of cake."

"If you're certain he remains in the city of your human body, you could slow him down."

"I'm open to any suggestions."

"Seek out imbalances in the elemental plane," Fire suggests. "Instead of releasing their tension to restore the balance, divert the pressure to fuel changes in your element."

"I thought I wasn't supposed to mess with the balance." That was the basic message Tremor and Quake drummed into my head over and again.

"In general, yes," Fire says. "But if you are careful and spread the imbalance over a larger area for a short period of time, the effect will be minimal."

"Then what do I do with it?"

"Use your imagination. What could you do to push earth into something that would affect Todd's fires?"

I stare at Fire's flickering humanoid shape. What influences fire?

"It's difficult for earth to contain fire," I say slowly. "Not without major upheaval. But I'm a fundamental. Can I partner with air elementals in the area, get them to use the energy in the imbalance to halt wind in the region? Without breeze to feed the flames, human firefighters could conquer a blaze with ease."

"Now you're thinking," Fire says with approval. "Get creative. Is there anything else you wanted to discuss? I have a wildfire in Australia that needs my attention."

I thank the fundamental and watch Fire's orange strands dissolve and flow southward. It's unfortunate that I can't find

Todd in the network, but at least I have a new skill. I hate Todd knowing more than me. I'm fifteen centuries old and a fundamental to boot, and he pulled out a new trick. It's galling.

Since I'm in the network already—and, let's face it, I have nowhere critical to be in the human world—I spread myself thin and sense for disturbances in the strands. It's a calming task, connecting and immersing myself in my element, and I bask in the sensation. Glimpses of other elementals whisk past, but I don't engage in conversation.

A snarl prods me out of my contemplative mood. I focus my conscious at the spot, and soon enough I'm examining the knot. A landslide is brewing, but it's stuck. A few earth strands of a mountain are tangled with blue threads of a cascading river that flows down its side. Two elementals argue near the knot.

"It's not my job to move for you," the earth elemental says grandly, its reddish-brown strands slowly twisting. "You're water, you change your course. It's what you're good at."

"One small strand is all you need to move," the water elemental says with a growl like churning rapids. "Work together to keep the balance, they always say."

"Yes, they do," I say, and the elementals' threads twitch with surprise. "Balance is everything, right? Work it out. I'll do a loop of the mountain. By the time I come back, I want this resolved."

The elementals send out wordless affirmations, and I float away. Will my task be that easy? It amuses me that elementals and humans are not so different. Ambition and laziness flow through the essences of each.

A bright grouping of clusters stops me in my tracks. I float toward the gathering of multicolored lauvan. It's clearly a small town nestled between two mountains and bordered by the heaving ocean. I examine the site, including the two elementals still arguing on the mountain's slope, and the whole picture resolves itself. Once the elementals sort out their differences, a landslide will crash upon the unsuspecting town. It's shaping up to be a big one, and by my best guess, half the town will be devastated.

Even through the lack of emotion in my current bodiless state, my horror at the loss of life pounds through. People die all the time, in every age of the world, but something about being directly responsible for mass destruction turns my stomach. It's hard to abide.

But what can I do? The balance must be maintained. I took this fundamental position to better the world, and I intend to excel at it for the sake of Minnie's memory. She died so that I could take this role on, after all. But what would Minnie say? Is it better to uphold the balance for the greater good, or save the townsfolk from certain death?

Perhaps there is a way to do both. Tremor won't approve, but if I keep my actions small, hopefully the balance will be only minimally affected.

A glance up the mountain assures me that the elementals are still arguing, but they could resolve their differences at any moment. I need to act fast. How can I save the town?

Wild ideas chase through my mind. Pushing up a berm to divert the landslide to a safer location would be inexplicable and far too grandiose to avoid detection by humans and elementals alike. Slowing the landslide would still result in destruction, and the arguing elementals need to see their fundamental performing his duties admirably to encourage them to do the same.

A warning to the townsfolk will have to suffice, but I have no physical body in this location, and time is of the essence. What form could a warning take? Roiling ocean threads catch my attention. This coastal town is well-attuned to the dangers of a tsunami. If I create a small earthquake to frighten them, surely they would run for the hills. As luck would have it, of the two mountains that cradle the town, the only one with roads is the one not affected by an upcoming landslide.

Enough planning. I need to act now.

I swoop under the town and twitch a few choice threads. A tremor wriggles clusters in the town. For good measure, I repeat the gesture.

Within a minute, a mass exodus of multicolored clusters is on the move, away from the pending landslide and up the other mountain. If I had lungs in this form, I would heave a sigh of relief.

Shaking strands in the corner of my vision make me whirl around. My earthquake occurred not a moment too soon. The elementals must have resolved their differences because a jumble of earth lauvan rockets down the slope. I flow out of the way and watch as the bubbling earth strands sweep over half of the town and cover it with brown. A few clusters are swept underneath the mass of rock and soil, but most humans escaped with their lives.

A warm fire ignites in me. It's a pale approximation of the pleasure of so many lives saved, but I recognize satisfaction when I feel it.

A twitch in the strands pulls my attention seaward. Above the shoreline, a knot has formed. How did that happen?

"Earth?" A flicker of auburn alerts me to Tremor's presence. "I felt your interference here. What happened?"

"I resolved a dispute between water and earth elementals," I say mulishly. I know where Tremor is going with her question, but I don't have to like it. The warm glow in my mind is replaced by uncertainty about the origin of the new knot.

Tremor takes in the situation within moments.

"You created an earthquake that unbalanced this region," she says. "Why?"

100

"It was just a little one. The landslide would have killed hundreds of people. I only warned them it was coming."

Tremor's consternation is palpable through the strands.

"You can't do that. I know it's hard to separate your feelings for these humans because you are partly one of them, but you must devote your whole self to being the fundamental. The world needs you undivided."

"Just help me fix it," I snarl.

Tremor silently acquiesces, and together we float toward the knot for a bout of untangling.

When the knot is gone, thanks to Tremor's efficient motions, the release of tension causes a large rogue wave to wash up on shore then filter back into the sea. I turn to her.

"Sorry," I say. "I'm trying to figure this out. It's hard."

"I would say I understand. But I don't, since I have no feelings for the humans you love. But I do understand that change is hard. If I can help, I will. You need only ask."

We part ways, and I fly back to my body. I'm not looking forward to entering the physical world again, and when I flow back to my body, the expected raw emotions hit me hard. I grip my hair, overcome by guilt over the few people who didn't evacuate the town before the landslide hit.

I wrestle with my overactive body in vain, then I pull out my phone for a distraction. Multiple texts and calls from Jen litter the screen. I press "call" and wait for her to pick up. It only takes one ring.

"Merry! Where are you? What the hell happened? The police called me in for questioning, and I didn't know what to say!"

"I hope you were truthful." I don't want Jen to get into trouble and have to run like me. I amend my statement. "As truthful as you can be while not mentioning elementals and immortality."

101

Jen lets out a disgruntled huff.

"I did my best. They didn't tell me much about what happened, so you'd better fill me in."

"Todd set me up." I lean against the tree trunk again, hoping it is strong enough to support the weight of my wearying life. "I chased after him, then he lit another fire and Kat Lee caught me there. She was already suspicious of me, and my presence checked enough boxes for her to haul me in. Obviously, I wasn't going to let that happen, so now I'm on the run with a new face."

"What? You're not leaving, are you?"

Jen sounds panicked. My bruised heart heals a little at her concern.

"Not yet. I still need to stop Todd. After that, who knows?"

"Come to my apartment," she orders. "Keep your disguise and use my place as a base. You need somewhere to go in this city. Then we can plan how to catch Todd. I'll call Alejandro and the others. We'll figure something out."

"You don't need to be involved. This is a fundamental thing, it doesn't concern you."

"Bull," she says, her tone vehement. "This concerns us because it concerns you. I don't care how depressed you feel, you are not alone in this. We always have your back, no matter if you're an ethereal spirit or a cocky warrior or a literature instructor. Do you hear me? We are always here for you."

I'm silent for a long moment, digesting her words. I know she means them, but I'm not sure if I'm a part of her world enough to warrant her concerns.

"I'll keep your offer in mind," I say at last.

"Do that." Jen sounds close to tears. "And you'd better turn up to Liam's grand opening this evening, even if you're wearing a different face. He needs his friends to support him."

I sigh but can't find an excuse not to come. With a different face, it's not difficult to evade capture, even if I am on the run.

"I'll be there."

CHAPTER XI

I pull up to the now-familiar street and park my blue bike out front. Liam's shop has undergone a dramatic change. Gone are the ugly newspapers that covered the windows. Inside, bright lights illuminate freshly painted walls with large mirrors surrounding soft mats that look perfect for throwing students to the ground, and I grin despite myself.

A crowd of about twenty people mill about inside, clutching paper cups and napkins with appetizers. Some of the faces I recognize: Jen, Alejandro, and Wayne with his girlfriend Anna. Liam's face glows with pride even through concern over the party's success.

I push the glass door open and enter. The scent of fresh paint and rubber assaults my nose. Jen approaches me with a brilliant smile.

"Welcome to the grand opening of School of the Sword," she says brightly. "Please, come in and grab some refreshments."

"Jen, it's me," I say quietly. "It's Merry."

She wraps me in a tight hug before letting me go and glancing at me critically.

"You couldn't be average for once, could you?" she says. "Never mind. How are you? Stupid question. What's the next step in finding Todd?"

"I'm still working on it. You said there was food?"

Jen huffs but leads me to the table. She whispers to Alejandro as she passes, and he follows us. I select a handful of crackers and cheese, suddenly ravenous. I don't remember the last time I ate.

"We're with you all the way," Alejandro says to me.

"Jen mentioned," I mumble through a mouthful of cracker.

"I mean it. We're ready to fight Todd, distract the police, whatever you need."

The swell of gratitude at Alejandro's unswerving loyalty nearly undoes me, but my raw emotions won't help me catch Todd and fulfill my fundamental duties. I mercilessly tamp down the feeling. I need to keep my friends at arm's length. It's for their own good, and for the good of the world.

"Thanks. I'll let you know if I need help."

My voice is cold even to my ears, and I wonder if I have overdone it when Alejandro blinks in surprise. Jen's face darkens, but before she can say more, Liam clears his throat from the center of the room.

"Hello. Can everyone hear me?" he says in a tentative voice. When heads nod, he smiles. "Great. Thanks for coming. This is the grand opening of School of the Sword. The school is a passion project of mine. I've spent years learning western martial arts." He glances at Alejandro and unsuccessfully forces his face into a serious expression. "But it's only recently that my love of the sword and all the history it brings with it has been rekindled. I wanted to share that joy with others, and so School of the Sword was born. We're starting small, but I have big plans for expansion. I have to thank a few people for their tremendous help: Jen for arranging sponsorship opportunities, Wayne and Merry for agreeing to teach, and Alejandro for pretty much everything."

The others smile widely as their names are called out, but I don't react. I haven't done anything yet to be thanked for, and Liam doesn't know my new face yet. Liam continues his speech.

"It's my dream that everyone who takes classes here will feel like family. I want to make this space a welcoming one for everyone, which is why one of the first classes we'll hold will be for an underprivileged youth program. If you wish to

105

donate, please get in touch with Alejandro. Thanks again and enjoy the refreshments. We'll start a demonstration shortly."

Liam finishes, the small crowd applauds, and chatter breaks out as he winds his way toward us. I reflect on Liam's program. All my friends are so entrenched in their human lives, and acting with integrity is so clear to them, unmuddied by the murky waters of elemental issues. I envy their certainty, and my solitude has never felt starker nor more unwelcome.

Someone must have pointed me out to Liam, for he stops in front of me and grips my shoulder briefly.

"Thanks for coming, Merry," he says quietly. "I know you have a lot going on. Anything I can do, just let me know."

I nod, although I have no intention of taking Liam up on his offer, because there is nothing he and the others can do.

"Who's doing the demonstration?" I ask to redirect the conversation.

"I had planned on me and Wayne," Liam says with a glint in his eyes. "But I'm open to challenges."

A burst of laughter escapes me.

"You think you're up for a challenge? Careful what you wish for." My good mood subsides, and I ponder the greater meaning of Liam's work here. "You've truly embraced your past, haven't you?"

"Is it that obvious?" He grins. "What gave it away?"

"I'm happy for you, that you found peace with it, and more, that you found your passion. It's—" I stop myself from blurting out the word *enviable*. "Inspiring. But I'll have to decline your challenge tonight. I have other pressing duties."

Liam looks downcast, but he rummages in his pocket for a slip of paper.

"Can you make these times?" he asks. "As a guest instructor?"

I take the offered paper and scan the dates reflexively,

although now that I have no classes—now that I have no life—I have all the time in the world beyond my fundamental duties. Again, I wonder what I'm doing pretending I'm still human. Surely, it would be a better use of my time to devote myself to my fundamental role. I have little left for me here, now that Kat Lee has ripped away the last semblance of normality I had left.

"I'll do my best," I say.

Liam nods.

"Thanks, Merry. I appreciate it."

I slip out after that, despite Jen's protestations—I was supposed to join them for dinner—but Liam's heartfelt thanks ring in my ears for long after.

I leave Liam's party like I have somewhere to go, but that's not true. My feet wander aimlessly until the shabby streets of the east side clean up into downtown proper. Shiny high-rises gleam in reflected streetlights, and curbside eateries burst with color and life.

I walk by, peering at the happy humanity inside each establishment, and what divides us feels far more substantial than glass. My chest aches, and I long for the blissful numbing of emotion that the network gives me.

A cluster of blue lauvan catches my eye, and my head whips around before I can think. A laughing man sips a bottled beer at a window table, and his sky-blue threads twitch in response to his mirth.

My heart sinks and I press on. I suppose there's no guarantee that Minnie will return as a woman, so every lead is worth investigating, but the man's strands were brighter than I expect new-Minnie's will be. With every successive lifetime, Minnie's strands reached a deeper shade of blue, and her last ones were navy.

I now have a goal for my evening, and in every restaurant window I gaze shamelessly at the patrons inside. None sport a shade of blue darker than a stellar's jay feather, and by the fifth block, I am too despondent to continue. Will I have to wait for Minnie to find me?

A sizzle of an idea ripples down my spine. Of course. The fundamentals said that Minnie will come back in the body of a dying person. Why am I looking for healthy people enjoying themselves, when I should be looking for a convalescent?

My feet pick up the pace, and I direct my steps to the nearest hospital. It's only a few blocks away, and I have to hold myself back from running to its brightly lit front doors.

It's too late for visiting hours, so I deftly twist my strands into passable scrubs and stride inside like I have somewhere urgent to be. I race up the stairs and down a hall—quiet in the evening—and a clipboard swiped from a shelf on the wall provides me with a prop. At every passing door, I peek inside.

Some patients are asleep, and some stare at me as I mutter to myself and pretend to tick something on my clipboard. One middle-aged woman sparks my interest with her blue strands, but they are the brilliant azure of a summer's sky, not nearly dark enough to be Minnie's new threads.

It takes an hour to comb the hospital—successfully dodging one suspicious nurse on the third floor—before I concede defeat. I walk out of the front doors and let my scrubs dissolve into regular clothes. Minnie hasn't returned to me in this hospital. I wish I could find her, not least because I could heal her injuries with my abilities. Wherever she is, I won't find her tonight.

If I don't have my human life, and I don't have Minnie,

what do I have? Waving brown strands spell the answer. I have my fundamental duties, always and forever. It might not bring me joy, but it gives me purpose, which is more than I can boast in any other facet of my life.

And my next priority as fundamental is finding Todd, since I'm uniquely positioned to search for him now that he is hidden in the elemental plane. That half-elemental thorn in my side is the only thing that's stopping me from moving to a new town. Minnie will find me, no matter where I go, and my life is over here. I can't hold onto my disguise forever. Finding Todd will give me the freedom to move on.

I kick the lid of an errant coffee cup out of my way then turn around and stride back to my motorbike. If I want to start a new life, one that isn't hampered by well-meaning friends and meddlesome cops nor constrained by tiring disguises, I need to buckle down and tackle the Todd problem. I know where he lives, so I'll start there. Any lead is better than a cold trail.

Todd's apartment is in a rundown four level block whose stucco is in desperate need of a paint job. At this hour, many of the windows glow in the darkness, some with lamplight, some with the blue of televisions. Todd's apartment on the second floor is dark, which is both a blessing and curse. His absence will give me a chance to search his apartment for clues, but if he were there currently, I could snatch him right now and be done with this.

A woman approaches the front door, and I seize my chance. My feet stride with a deceptively quick saunter until I'm right behind her.

"Sorry, I forgot my keys," I say when she turns to look at me with a startled expression. "I'm staying with Todd on the second floor for a week. Lovely city, Vancouver. I'm really enjoying my visit."

Disarmed by my babbling and smile, she fumbles with her keys at the door and stammers something about the city's waterfront. I nod encouragingly and hold the door open for her like a gentleman.

Once she disappears into the elevator, I open the door to a stairwell and slowly climb two flights. I want the woman to have plenty of time to enter her own suite in case she and Todd share a floor. In the second level hallway, I pause at the row of identical doors. Which suite is Todd's? The only other time I visited, I peeked in by climbing onto a dumpster.

It must be the third door on the left. I knock then flatten myself against the wall to avoid detection through the spyhole. If Todd is home and can open the door for me, it will save me time. Locks don't stop me, but they are fiddly and frustrating.

Another door clicks open across the hall, and loud reggae music blares out. I try for a grin to put the heavyset man in a cotton tank top at ease. He is startled but not suspicious.

"I thought I'd surprise Todd," I say. "Guess he's not home."

"Friend of his, are you?" the man says. He scratches his stomach and peers down the hall. "I thought I heard my wife coming back, but I guess it was just you. Todd doesn't live here anymore."

My heart sinks. My search for Todd in the physical world will prove much harder if I have no leads.

"I must have misheard his moving date," I improvise. "I was going to help him pack, but I guess I'll offer to unpack at his new place instead. I can't remember where he ended up, there were a few choices."

"Some swanky place in Coal Harbor, I heard." The man

sniffs his envy and distaste. "The Haven building. I only know because he wouldn't stop bragging about it and the ocean views." The man yawns and nods at me then retreats to his suite and closes the door.

I don't bother picking the lock of Todd's old apartment. I have a fresh lead, and it's far more promising than this empty set of rooms. If the Coal Harbor clue doesn't pan out, I can always come back here to investigate.

The Haven building is an intimidating expanse of glass and steel, fronted by sweeping concrete steps and a large fountain turned off at this time of year. Luckily, it takes far more than grandeur to intimidate me. I swing open the door like I own the place and stride with measured steps across an echoing lobby toward the doorman's desk. He glances at me from the pages of his novel.

"Can I help you, sir?" he says with a beady-eyed look.

I lean forward and wrap my fingers around the mustard strands that float freely around the man.

"I'm here to see Todd Holland. No need to ring up. I want to surprise him. You can forget I was here."

The man nods with a glazed look, and I release his strands. Quickly, before he recovers from my manipulation, I enter the elevator behind him and shut the door.

Now, what? It's a big building, and Todd could be anywhere. I curse myself for my haste with the doorman. It would have been simple to extract Todd's suite number from the docile man.

Strands dangle from the elevator buttons, and I peer closer. Some people must have shed their strands when they pressed their button, from excitement or age, and my eyes scan the colors for a clue. A peach-colored thread hangs from the fourteenth button, and my cheeks lift in a grim smile.

Todd's doorhandle is similarly easy to spot—both silver and orange strands dangle from the lever—and I quietly fiddle with the lock until it clicks open. I soundlessly slip into the apartment and suppress a whistle.

Counters and hardwood gleam in the moonlight, and vaulted ceilings soar above my head. The main room is massive, and it leads to further rooms beyond. Todd has set himself up very nicely indeed. The extortion business must be booming.

Now that I am alone, I release the strands of my disguise with a sigh of relief. It takes effort to maintain a transformation.

A cold breeze twists my head around. The balcony door is open. Is someone here? I creep to the sliding door and peek around the edge. The balcony wraps around this corner suite with views of diamond-sparkled ocean expanse and the lights of West Vancouver across the inlet.

A voice makes my heart nearly beat out of my chest. Todd's shadowy form stands at the corner of the railing. His arms are outstretched, and he holds a glimmering rope of air strands in his hands. The swaying humanoid shape of an elemental rises from the cable. I hold my breath to listen.

"We need to ramp things up," the elemental's whispery voice says. "The only way I'll level up is to make a bigger impact. I'm tired of managing the local onshore breeze."

"We both have goals, Ailu," Todd says. My eyes widen. The elemental is Ailu, my former air elemental contact. I haven't connected with him for months, although I introduced him to Todd. "What wind do you want to manage?"

"Hurricane season in the south," Ailu answers promptly.

"The area you call the Caribbean. So much power there! But to qualify, I have to prove that I can work well with others. Hurricanes are a group thing."

"Ha, that's why you agreed to work with me." Todd snorts. "You don't play well with other elementals, is that it? Works for me. Hope the hurricane boss counts slumming with a half-human as proof that you can cooperate."

"I hope so," Ailu says grimly. "They don't have to know the details, though. I have ways to prove my cooperation with you without exposing the specifics. You're right, my list of allies is thin. Once we complete our agreed-upon fire show, I will contact the hurricane group. But, until then, our tasks have been too small to mention. Hence, my request to step it up."

"Yeah, sounds good." Todd rubs his nose on his sleeve and sniffs. "I like seeing what I'm capable of. I'll keep doing the small jobs—the money's too good to pass up—but I want to stretch my legs. I'm done with being small potatoes. It's time people showed me some respect. Give me a few days to prepare for the spectacle on my end. You're going to keep helping me with the arson, though, right? Your techniques really boost the power of my fire. Something about us working together on different planes."

"If you insist. As long as we create our grand spectacle soon."

My mind reels from the revelations. Ailu and Todd together are creating fires far more potent than either could light on his own. That cross-plane partnership is somehow affecting local strands and creating problems with the balance.

Ailu and Todd's partnership can't be allowed to continue. The mixing of elemental and human isn't good for the balance, and it isn't good for the world. Ailu and Todd need to be kept apart for good.

But if the mixing of elemental and human is toxic, what

113

does that say about me?

My human life is a cliff crumbling into the crashing waves of my fundamental side. I'm retreating from my friends, I can't attend my work because of my wanted status, my wife sacrificed herself for the balance that the elemental world strives to maintain, and there is little left for me. Soon, I will be an empty husk of a human, only existing to serve the world of the elements.

And suddenly, fiercely, that scenario doesn't appeal. My mind floods with memories of being bodiless, when I thought I could become a pure elemental and then discovered my extreme attachment to my body and my human life. Am I so keen to try again? Because on the path I'm on, that future feels inevitable.

When my fully human Minnie returns to me—and I've been promised that she will—do I want to welcome her into a warm, human embrace? Or will she join me in a cold, empty existence devoid of light and laughter, existing only to serve the balance?

Because as much as I try to fulfill my fundamental duties, as much as I appreciate the stripping away of emotion in the network, I am not fully elemental and never have been. My roots are firmly planted on Earth, the physical world of my birth and life. I can't give that up.

I can't give up.

CHAPTER XII

This revelation hits me in an instant, but I push the contemplation aside for a time when I can explore it at leisure. For now, Todd is within my grasp. Even if I wish to embrace my human side, the fact remains that I am Earth, and my fundamental role is crucial for the wellbeing of the world. I might not be as keen to throw myself wholeheartedly into my fundamental duties, but there's no denying that they need to be done. Todd is my problem to solve, and solve him I will.

But I'm tired of relying solely on my elemental talents. I've survived for fifteen hundred years partly on the strength of my physical skills, and it's time to deal with human Todd in a human way. If I know him at all—and I've always seen myself in him—then he will expect me to attack with the power of the elements.

I rush out the door to grapple Todd into submission. Of course, a few well-placed yanks of lauvan will cement the deal, but physical combat is more my forte than Todd's.

Todd doesn't know what hits him. With a cry, he's on the tile floor with me on top of him, but I don't have long to celebrate. A freight-train's worth of air wallops me in the face, and I spin off Todd and slide the full length of the balcony. My body come to a crunching halt at the railing, and I sit, stunned.

Todd scrambles up and dusts off his overcoat.

"I thought that technique you taught me hid my thread signature from Merry," he yells at the breeze where Ailu lurks. "Now I have to move again, unless I kill him now, and I don't want to deal with his body. How did he find me?"

"Not everything is solved by lauvan," I croak.

Todd sneers at me.

"Whatever. Elemental powers are clearly superior to

measly human abilities. Stay away from me, Merry. If you're not with me, you're against me. I don't care if you're a fundamental or a king or the lord of the underworld. You're in my way. Take this failure as a lesson to turn a blind eye in the future, or you might not be so lucky next time."

"Is that a threat?" I shake my head to clear it and wish I hadn't when the world spins sickeningly. "I'm going to stop you, no matter what it takes."

"It's like that, is it?" Todd taps his toe in thought, while I frantically mash strands around my head to fix my vertigo. "In that case, it's on. Do your worst because I sure as hell am going to do mine."

I leap up, heedless of my swimming head, but Todd laughs and throws himself off the balcony. I rush to the railing and gaze, dumbfounded, when Todd rises on a current of howling wind and soars over the dark strait.

I slide to the tiles again. I'm angry beyond endurance and sick to my stomach from the blow to my head and fear of Todd's retaliation. What is Todd's worst? His imagination is limited, but with Ailu on his side, what will they dream up?

It takes me a solid ten minutes to massage the knots from my skull, but by the time my lauvan flow freely, I know a few things.

One, that Ailu and Todd's partnership upsets the balance under each fire they set. Somehow, their cross-plane devilries affect the delicate balance, and the only way to stop it is to prevent them from working together. Ailu is a powerful enough elemental that he can hide his signature in the elemental plane, and he taught Todd the same trick. Can Air restrain the errant elemental if Ailu can't be found? Forcing Ailu into dormancy would solve our problems today, but I wouldn't put it past Todd to find another ally in his quest for recognition. I will contact Air about Ailu soon, but the only way to stop half-elemental Todd's cross-plane disruptions is to deal with him in the physical world.

Two, the elemental plane and the physical world shouldn't be connected in such a close way. The fundamentals of old had it right when they prevented elementals from freely crossing into the physical world. If the balance must be maintained, then the two sides should stay as separate as possible.

And that leads me to the third thing I know: my human side is being swallowed up by my fundamental nature. The two sides can't coexist peacefully. I don't know how I can achieve a separation, but I need to figure it out before my humanity is lost forever.

What sort of threat does Todd think would affect me? I review our interactions to date, and my mind freezes in horror. He sees me as a do-gooder, trying to save innocents, trying to keep my friends safe.

My chest aches again, but this time I don't want to numb the pain. That ache means that I am alive, and I am human. It means I care, and that I have someone to care about. If Todd threatens my friends, I will need to harness my fear and anger and channel it toward taking him down. I can't afford to lose sight of what's important, not when I'm the one standing between my friends and whatever horrors Todd can dream up.

The balance of the world is paramount, but the balance within myself can't be ignored. Alejandro is right: although I fulfill my fundamental duties in her honor, Minnie wouldn't want me to be consumed by them. But I can't be a fundamental while still clinging to my human life. Something has to give.

What are my options? Slowly, the recollection of my first

conversation with the other fundamentals floats to the top of my mind.

A new fundamental can be made, but it takes time.

Hope flares in my chest. I could find another elemental to take my place. It might take time, but the possibility is there. My body lightens with the hope of freedom from this task, and I realize how much the responsibility weighs upon me.

Nothing is instant, of course, and the greater good of the world comes first. I will pursue a replacement for my position, but until then, I will uphold my end of the bargain. My fundamental duties will not waver, even as I try to claw back what's left of my human life. I can maintain both while I transition away from the elemental world and allow the separation between planes once more.

My head is clear now, in more ways than one, and I exit Todd's apartment with a purposeful spring in my step. I have another mission now, but this is one I feel passionate about. Releasing my fundamental duties to another is an intoxicating thought.

The doorman looks puzzled as I leave, as if he's never seen me before, but I merely wave and continue walking. The concrete steps before the high rise are too exposed for my purposes, so I hop on my bike and gun it to Stanley Park, a mere minute down the road. Here, I can sequester myself in the darkness of the trees while I enter the network.

I seek out Air's distinctive threads. The fundamental is mercifully close by, and I halt in the earth strands under a rushing torrent of air threads.

"Earth," Air says and coalesces into a human shape to speak with me. "What troubles you?"

"The half-elemental Todd is allied with Ailu, an air elemental that controls the onshore breeze near my physical body's home. Their cooperation between planes is what is

118

causing the disruptions. Can you control Ailu somehow? Send him into dormancy? At least stop him from leveling up based on his actions here?"

Air's sigh holds the force of a gale.

"Fundamentals function as grand coordinators and don't have the power of absolute rule. 'Leveling up', as you call it, happens without my oversight, and once done, the elemental becomes unrecognizable as its former self. Also, if this Ailu can hide in the network, then it will take me some time to find the elemental. I will send emissaries to search, but the process will not be swift."

I nod my strand head.

"I suspected as much. I still need to deal with Todd. But whatever you can do on your end will help."

I float back to my body but don't merge with the chocolate brown human strands yet. I have a question that I need earth elementals to answer. I send out a summons among the colorful filaments of the elemental plane, and within moments, Tremor and Quake float toward me.

"Greetings, Earth," Tremor says to me.

I skip pleasantries, too eager to get to my question.

"How can an elemental be prepared to become a fundamental, if not already in the line of succession?"

Sensations of surprise emit from each elemental.

"We could find out, I suppose," Tremor says. "It hasn't been done for a while."

"Not for Earth, you mean," Quake says. "It happens quite frequently for Fire. They're constantly being reborn. Not as often for the big bosses, of course, but still more often than Earth."

"I believe it involves a similar stretching process as we performed on you," Tremor adds. "It takes longer, and a gradual transfer of power and knowledge must occur at the same time. We couldn't prepare one for your position quickly enough."

"How long is longer?"

Quake gave the mental equivalent of a shrug.

"For Earth? I don't know. Stretching an elemental to hold enough power is an artificial process, unlike leveling up, and since it doesn't happen often, who can say?"

"You need an elemental with enough power," I repeat, thinking furiously. "Tell me, can two elementals share the power and responsibility?"

Tremor and Quake are silent for a moment.

"Perhaps," Tremor replies slowly. "I have heard of merges before."

"What are you getting at, Earth?" Quake asks with suspicion.

There is no reason to keep my idea a secret from these two. They have been with me every step of the way during this elemental journey, and I trust them completely. Besides, I need them.

"I want to transfer the power of Earth to another," I say bluntly. "I'm not a good candidate for this responsibility. I'm doing my best, but a half-human in this position is like hammering a square peg into a round hole. I know the process of preparing another for the power might be a long one, but I also know that it can be done."

The others are silent for a long moment. A hum of unformed questions floats toward me.

"You're a great fundamental," Quake says finally. "I don't understand why you're saying this."

"You get it, don't you, Tremor?" I ask her. "You've had to school me in proper fundamental ways more than once. I can't let go of my human nature, and I've realized that I don't want to. Earth should be someone who puts the balance of the world

120

beyond everything else. I'm trying, but I don't know for how long I can do that without losing myself."

Tremor sighs.

"Are you certain about this?"

"Yes."

"Are you serious?" Quake demands. "You're encouraging him to transition out of being the fundamental? We worked so hard to get him here. And who is supposed to take over the role? Who is suitable?"

"I have an idea for that," I say. "That's why I asked about the merging. What if you and Tremor jointly took on the role?"

Quake scoffs then grows silent. Tremor's strands twitch and shiver.

"I don't know," she whispers. "It might work."

"I've never heard of a merged fundamental," Quake says.

"Just because it hasn't been done, doesn't mean it can't be." Tremor's strands grow firm. "It would greatly speed the transitioning process if we could pool our strength as one. Of course, that means I would be tied to you forever."

Tremor's voice takes on a teasing quality, and Quake's strands puff in mock-outrage.

"You should be so lucky." Quake's focus returns to me. "What about the other fundamentals? I don't know how they'll take it."

"Surely, Earth has some autonomy from the others?" I ask. "Leave the fundamentals to me. This is the right path, I'm sure of it. The only question is, how do we do this?"

"Stretching," Tremor says to no one's surprise. "You can help with that, Earth. I'll ask around about merging procedures. Also, we'll have to find replacements for our own duties." Her voice takes on a softer tone. "I'm touched, Earth, that you think we are worthy of this great honor."

"You've earned it." I move toward her, and I can't help the

grin in my voice at the upcoming preparations. "Ready to stretch?"

It's the middle of the night when I finally emerge from the network. Stretching Tremor and Quake took many hours, and then I took time to hide my strands from elemental sight. Now that Todd is onto me, I don't want to give him any edge. My body shudders from the cold, and the effort it takes me to walk from my lonely bike on an empty side street to my apartment is immense. The only thing that keeps me warm is the fire of my new goal.

At my apartment, I enter through the patio door to avoid a security camera set up by the police to monitor my movements. The police have visited—evident from my door's broken latch and the bedroom's open drawers—but my place is so sparse that I can hardly tell they rifled through my belongings. I fall into bed fully clothed and wrap myself in blankets until the shivering ceases and sleep takes me. The process would be far swifter with a pair of warm arms around me, and my mind fills with thoughts of Minnie as I drift into sleep.

CHAPTER XIII

Dreaming

I've chewed the last bit of mutton from the bones, and I idly pick apart bread and sop up a puddle of juices from the table. The campaign season will start soon—scouts have spotted Saxons on the southern coast—and warriors have left their winter dwellings to gather at Arthur's villa in preparation. Consequently, the midday meal is more populated than usual, and Guinevere hasn't yet eaten in her busyness with directing serving maids.

When her eye sweeps past me, I wave her over.

"Guinevere, sit for a moment. Eat some of this mutton. It's very good."

I push the dish toward her, but she shakes her head with a frazzled look.

"I'll eat later. There's so much to prepare. I think everyone has eaten, so I'll tell the servants to clean up." She looks around with a start. "Wait, have you seen Elian? He'll have to go without a meal if he doesn't get here soon."

I rise to my feet with a stretch.

"Stop fussing, Guinevere. I'll find him."

She throws me a dark look and retreats to another table. I chuckle and saunter to the door of the great hall. Arthur's villa, while extensive, boasts only a few places to look for a wayward warrior. It won't take long to sniff out Elian.

It's hard to move too quickly after my heavy meal, and I stroll through the muddy yard with a satisfied stomach and contented mind. I'm not looking forward to meals in the camp. While our cooks aren't bad, considering the conditions they work in, the villa's kitchens produce a far superior repast.

Shouts and the thud of wood on wood draws my attention, and I direct my steps to the stables. A group of young boys, no older than six or seven summers, battle each other with sticks on the far side. They shout with glee and tiny ferocity. Was I ever that small? It's hard to imagine.

Elian corrects one boy's stance then releases him to continue his fight. When he catches my eye, he grins and walks toward me.

"I was passing by when I saw them having a mock battle. Their form was so terrible that I couldn't leave without saying something."

I laugh.

"And are they improving?"

Elian points at the eldest pair, whose intent faces show their concentration.

"They're not flailing much anymore. You should have seen them before I got here."

"But their footwork could use some correction."

I stride forward and grab the back of the nearest boy's shirt. He looks up in surprise.

"Lighter on your feet," I say. "The enemy will find it easy to best you if your feet are leaden. And swing with your whole body, not just your arm."

I hold his shoulder to demonstrate, and the boys watch avidly. When I back away, they engage with each other once more. This time, they practically dance on light feet, and their shoulders move with their thrusts.

Elian and I share a grin over our new students.

"Guinevere sent me to look for you," I say. "She says you'll be without a meal if you don't hurry up. The mutton is worth rushing for."

"Thanks, Merlin. I'd better run." Elian turns to the boys and shouts over their noise. "Good work, everyone. The kitchen will have bread for your efforts if you tell them I sent you."

The boys stop their fighting, give a ragged cheer, and race toward the villa.

CHAPTER XIV

Early the next morning I jolt awake, as buzzed as if I swallowed a jug of coffee. The events of last night race through my memory in double speed. Todd—Ailu—stretching—transfer. I won't be a fundamental anymore.

My body feels lighter than air. While the role of fundamental gave me much-needed purpose during the dark weeks after Minnie's death, it was too much for one half-elemental. I was losing myself, and now that I want myself, I'm scrabbling frantically to keep my human side intact.

But I need to deal with Todd before I lose the powers of a fundamental. He's turning out to be quite powerful, especially with Ailu on his side. If I want a decent chance at beating him, I need to call on all my elemental and human wiles. Finding Todd is a human job, and I can't do it alone.

Being human means leaning on others. I leap out of bed and resolve to visit Wayne right away. He's handy with online searching, something my medieval mind never learned well, and he could be invaluable in looking for Todd. If I'm to embrace my human side, I'd better start mending bridges with my friends.

I throw on clean clothes, shove stale bread into my mouth, don my disguise once more, and race to my motorbike via the patio door. Minutes later, I screech to a stop in front of Wayne's place. He rents the middle floor of a large heritage house, and I leap up the steps two at a time. He answers the door after my fervent knocking, his shirt half-buttoned and a toothbrush hanging out of his mouth.

"Merry?" he says through a mouthful of toothpaste. "What are you doing here? Come in, let me spit."

When Wayne finally emerges, dressed and toothbrush-free,

I'm nearly dancing with impatience in his living room.

"Wayne, I need your help."

Wayne looks surprised.

"I'm glad to hear it. What's up?"

The words tumble out of me as if I have been keeping them locked away for too long.

"I need to find Todd and stop him, he's upsetting the balance and I'm the only fundamental who can do it because he's hiding his signature in the network and the others can't track him, and I'm partly human so I can look for him on our side. I need to do it soon, though, because I'm the only one who can and I plan to transfer my fundamental powers to other elementals and get rid of this altogether, then I can be myself again, and I realized I've been drifting away, and I'm sorry."

I take a breath, surprised by my outpouring of words. Wayne's lips are tight with suppressed emotion.

"Apology accepted," he says finally and claps me on the shoulder. "Glad to have you back. So, you want to find Todd?"

"That's the plan. He's a thorn in my side that I need to pluck out. Oh, and he's in league with Ailu, my former air elemental ally. I hesitate to use the word friend, because I'm not sure that elementals can feel enough emotion to have friends." I consider Tremor and Quake and amend my words. "Perhaps that's not true, but certainly Ailu is an acquaintance only."

Wayne taps his fingers on his thigh, and his mouth twists in thought.

"You know, someone logged into our website this morning using Anna's username, but she was with me at the time."

Wayne's website is a database that he built to record the memories of his and the others' past lives. I half-heartedly filled out portions of my life, unwilling to spend the copious time needed to document my one-and-a-half thousand years in the world and disliking the bittersweet memories it dredged up.

127

The others, however, took to it like ducks to water, and there are reams of information linking them to each other through the ages.

The site is password protected, so only Wayne, Alejandro, Jen, Liam, Anna, and I can access it. I frown.

"Did she give the password to someone else?"

"She swears she didn't, but she keeps her password on a sticky note beside her computer in our library." Wayne huffs his displeasure. "I've tried to talk her out of it. Do you think someone broke in?"

"I don't know how else they could have got the password." I move toward the door. "I'm going to check it out."

Wayne grabs his keys and coat from a side table.

"I'll come too. Then we can talk further about finding Todd."

Wayne follows me in his car behind my bike. The apartment I rented, where we store the books liberated from March Feynman's library of spirits and the occult, is only minutes away. Wayne unlocks the front door, and I take the stairs two steps at a time.

The library is quiet and carries the scent of old books. I glance around the room for clues, and Wayne moves to the laptop on a nearby folding table.

"The sticky note is gone," he says with a strained voice. "And look at this."

I walk swiftly to his side and follow the direction of his pointing finger. A book lies open on the table, pages ripped out of the center. A telltale peach-colored thread dangles from the open book like a ribbon bookmark. I flip the book over to look at the title.

"Todd was here," I say heavily. "Looks like he wanted to know more about his element. This book discusses the anthropology of fire gods among different cultures."

128

Wayne curses.

"How do you know it was Todd?"

"Lauvan." I flick away the offending strand and slam the book shut. "I guess we know who logged into the website. But why? What could he do with the information?"

"I don't know. It really has no practical purpose for anyone except us."

Wayne looks around the desk for more clues while I ponder Todd's motivations. He straightens from his bent position with a crumpled napkin in his hand.

"What do you bet this is Todd's?" he says in triumph. "And there's a logo on it. At least we can find out where he went this morning. Any clues are better than none."

I peer at the logo of a swirly loaf of bread in moss green.

"I don't recognize it. Do you?"

"No, of course not."

"Then we're out of luck again."

Wayne pulls out his phone with a shake of his head at me.

"Merry. Get with the twenty-first century. A simple image search will tell us what we need to know."

"You can do that?"

Modern technology never ceases to surprise me.

"You bet. Give me a few minutes."

Wayne sits in the chair before the computer, head bent over his phone, and I wander to the kitchen to check for food in the fridge. I'm ravenous, and when I reflect on my eating habits of late, my stomach rumbles in displeasure. I wasn't taking care of myself as I retreated from the human world, wrapping myself in the numbing blanket of my fundamental duties. Minnie would be shaking her head if she were here.

Like a lance to my chest, Minnie's absence leaves me gasping. It's been almost two months, and just when I think the pain is softening, a thought or scent can rip open the wound anew. The longing to descend into the network and escape this emotion is nearly overwhelming, and I clench my fingernails into my palms to resist the impulse. I'm already hanging onto my human life by a thread. I need to focus on rebuilding what I have left before my fundamental duties swallow me whole.

Besides, I'll need to check into the network soon. The prospect of future relief eases the tightness in my chest. I can wait a few hours.

"Got it," Wayne says when he finds me in the kitchen munching a dry bagel that Anna must have left here. He passes me a piece of paper with an address on it in his loopy scrawl. "This is the bakery. It's not a chain, so he definitely visited this location. Likely this morning, given the napkin. It's not much, but at least we can ask the staff if they remember anything."

"This is brilliant. I had no clues otherwise." I stand and stretch my arms to the ceiling before popping the last bite of bagel in my mouth. "Thanks, Wayne. I'll investigate right away. With any luck, he's staying in the neighborhood."

"I can come with you," Wayne offers, but I shake my head.

"You have work. Finding the location was great, but I have it from here."

Doubt wreathes his face.

"We're here for you, Merry. I know we're not as flashy as elementals, but us old humans have our uses."

"I know." But when I have to pull out my abilities, Wayne and the others will get in the way. Until I relinquish my fundamental nature, some distance is necessary. "Wish me luck."

The address that Wayne gave me is to a short row of shops

across from a dense cluster of houses on a treed side street. The bakery with its distinctive green logo nestles snugly in the center, its neon "open" sign lit. I flip my kickstand in front of the middle house across from the bakery. It's a clapboard structure whose gray paint has seen better days. My only plan is to find Todd—take him down, if I'm lucky—but now that I am confronted by a row of blank doors and a shop unlikely to have answers, I'm reconsidering my lack of strategy. Twice, now, Todd has escaped my clutches. Perhaps I need a more thoughtful approach.

But I've always been one for living in the moment. I'll wing it. Perhaps someone here has noticed Todd hanging around.

While I'm deciding which door to hammer on first, a taxi pulls over. A familiar voice hails me.

"Merlo!"

Alejandro flings some cash at the taxi driver and races toward me. He skids to a stop at my side, despite the disguise I donned again at Wayne's house.

"I'm here to help," he pants. "Wayne called. What's the plan?"

I gaze at him without answering immediately. Wayne called Alejandro, and without thinking, he dropped everything and ran to my side because he knew I needed help and wouldn't ask for it.

I don't deserve friends like this.

"Well?" he says. "How are we finding Todd?"

"I'm sorry I've been distant lately," I croak out. "Well, more of a cold bastard, if I'm being honest."

Alejandro waves my words away.

"You can get soft later if you have to. Focus, Merlo. What's the plan?"

I nod and push aside my gratitude and the cold shivers that threaten to race down my back at the thought of almost giving up on my humanity. Alejandro's right. Todd is the priority right now.

I open my mouth to speak—not that I have a grand plan—then a gentle tug latches onto me. The sensation travels through my lauvan into my body, and it grows more insistent with every passing second. Is something wrong in the network?

"Give me half a minute," I say to Alejandro. "I need to check something. Consider how to question the neighbors in this row of houses about seeing Todd while I'm unavailable."

Alejandro looks confused, but I ignore him, close my eyes, and descend into the network.

Quake is there, waiting for me. Distress pours off him in waves.

"We need you," he says without preamble. "The plate below here is terribly unstable. The elemental in charge of releasing pressure was negligent. Tremor dismissed the elemental into dormancy, but we have to fix the issue while she brings the next elemental up to speed."

"This isn't a great time," I begin, but Quake's distress infects me too. "Never mind. I can do both. Let's get you started with the fix, then I'll come back and check in."

Quake doesn't say anything, but his consternation is palpable. He leads me directly underground, through thick earth strands and pockets of water threads, deep into the mantle. The snarl is evident from a distance, with the farthest-reaching tangles spreading out from a core of knots. It pulses with sick energy.

"All right, let's dig in," I say with false enthusiasm. I'm acutely aware of Alejandro waiting beside my inert body, but I can't deny the need for my presence here.

Quake swoops around the bundle of knots, loosening them with impressive speed. I tackle a few particularly nasty ones then rise to my body.

When I enter it with my customary gasp for air, Alejandro looks relieved and drags me by my arm behind a fence.

"You're back."

"I need to return to the network shortly," I say to Alejandro. My mind whirls with my two tasks. "There's a crisis there."

"I saw him in a window," Alejandro hisses. "Todd's in the gray house."

My heart leaps uncomfortably, but my fists clench in anticipation. It's time for Todd to face the music. And, with Alejandro on my side, maybe I can finally defeat him.

"Let's run through the front door," I say. It's hardly an inspired move, but I'm eager to do anything. The niggling worry of the plate below my feet doesn't help my concentration. "Corner him."

"You start," Alejandro says. "I'll slash his tires first. Make sure he can't get away quickly."

My mind flits to Todd's flying abilities, thanks to his ally Ailu, but I don't dissuade Alejandro. Covering our bases isn't a bad plan. I would feel stupid if Todd really did squeal away in a puff of exhaust.

"Meet me inside when you're done. Wait, I need a second in the network."

I can't ignore the niggling feeling any longer, and I close my eyes to descend once more. The knot is still there with Quake frantically untangling it.

"Good, you're back," he pants. "Quickly. I don't know how much longer we have."

My phantom heart sinks. The knot still pulses with tension, perhaps worse than before. What will happen if we don't release it? Feverishly, I dive into the knot and yank apart strands until a tugging draws me back to my body.

"I slashed the tires," Alejandro hisses when I regain

133

hearing. "But Todd saw me. Now's our chance. Quick!"

I follow Alejandro's lead, half of my attention still on the throbbing knot below me. I must go back, but I must also catch Todd. This might be my last real chance. Wayne could pull another fantastic find out of nowhere, but I doubt it. Once Todd is gone from here, he might disappear until his next big upheaval, and my efforts will come too late. Who might die because I don't catch him today?

But I must also balance finding Todd with my fundamental duties. If I don't take care of the knot, far worse things will happen to the world. I can't give up the bigger picture for one life. I'll just have to figure out how to do both.

Todd bursts from the front door, hands swinging wildly. He must look ridiculous to anyone else, but to me he wields weapons of great power. Air lauvan gather in his fists, and he launches clusters of them in our direction.

"Down!" I shout and push Alejandro to the ground. A second later, a roaring gale hits our heads and backs with the force of a blow.

I don't waste time. My fingers search for loose strands and yank with intention. Instantly, Todd is thrown off his feet when the ground under him buckles and strains.

"Now you're playing with the big boys," Todd yells once he regains his feet. His hands work so quickly they are almost blurred, and silver strands bundle around his fists. "Back to your elemental tricks, are you?"

I dive to the side when Todd releases his lauvan bundles. With a screech of metal, a car behind me bears the brunt of Todd's attack. The dented door makes my blood run cold, but I use my proximity to the ground to pour intention into brown earth strands.

Todd flips into the air as the ground underfoot jerks him like a flipped pancake. Air strands catch him before he smacks into the pavement. With a growl, his hands burst into flame.

Movement behind Todd catches my eye, but I'm careful not to look Alejandro's way.

"What are you going to do with that?" I jeer to keep Todd's attention on me. "Fry some bacon?"

Alejandro leaps toward Todd from behind and grabs both his forearms in a firm grip. Todd's surprise is comical, and the flames on his hands die. Quicker than Todd can react, Alejandro wraps his hands around Todd's fingers. I don't hang around to see more. With Todd's hands contained, his lauvan-manipulation is limited. Alejandro can handle him while I check out the brewing catastrophe below our feet.

I dive into the network. Quake flies around the knot, untangling what he can with frantic motions.

"It's too much," he pants. "I can't do it by myself."

"I'll take over. Gather every nearby earth elemental you can find so they can help."

"What about their tasks?"

"This is more important," I say in between knots. "Their tasks will last a few minutes without supervision, surely. You leave your assignments frequently to help me."

"I'm part of a group that manages a fault line. Your request is unusual, that's all."

"Do we have time for you to yammer about it?" I yank a thread free of the pulsing tangle. "Go!"

Quake disappears, leaving me with the unenviable task of thwarting this disaster. If unchecked, how big of an earthquake would this cause?

Shortly, Quake returns with a train of elementals of all shades of brown.

"Get to work," I tell them. "Quickly. I need to fight another fire in the physical world."

"Fire?" Quake sounds confused.

135

"Not an actual fire, a—never mind. Just work." Another thought occurs to me, courtesy of my chat with Fire. "Funnel the tension you release from the knots into the area under my body, all right? I need all the ammunition I can get to take down Todd."

I rise to my physical form where it crouches on the grass. When my eyes clear, Alejandro's prone body lies before me.

CHAPTER XV

My heart squeezes, and I rush to his side.

"I'm okay." He grunts in pain, contradicting his words. "Todd ran that way."

My fingers deftly twist the knot above a wound on his side that slowly seeps thick red blood while I scan the street for Todd. He races toward the far sidewalk where a jogger runs with a sweaty face and earbuds firmly planted in her ears.

Alejandro pushes me away.

"I'm fine now," he says in a stronger voice. "Go!"

A quick glance at Alejandro's neatly knitted wound convinces me that he won't bleed out. That will have to do. I leap to my feet and chase after Todd. He looks over his shoulder, and his eyes widen at my approach. Swifter than I can react, he twists air strands near him.

With a shriek, the jogger rises into the air and dangles above Todd's head. Her earbuds fall out and her ponytail dangles from behind her terrified face.

"Back away," Todd shouts at me. "Or I'll hurt her. That wouldn't sit well with your do-gooder nature, would it?"

A sharp tug of my strands alerts me to a development in the network. I don't have time to deal with Todd right now. He is only one man, and a whole city's stability hangs in the balance. But if I don't trap Todd now, how will I ever find him again? I need time to perform my fundamental duties.

A flash of brilliance directs my hands. With effort, I pull on nearby earth threads. Faster than Todd can move, the ground surrounding him shakes and splits open. Thanks to the extra energy from Quake's redirection, progress is swifter than I dreamed. Dirt shoots in a circle from cracks in the pavement and creates a crumbling dome of brown soil that encapsulates my opponent.

There. That should trap him until I'm ready. With the extra power infused into the dome, it will take more than Todd to break through. The uncertain fate of the jogger troubles my conscience, but it's either her or the entire city. I must be the fundamental until Tremor and Quake are ready to take up the mantle. Until then, I must put the greater good over the fate of one, at least for a little while longer. Hopefully, Todd was bluffing. I close my eyes and descend into the network.

Tremor has joined Quake and the lesser elementals, and a positive hive of activity surrounds the knot. It still pulses angrily, and the tension is on a knife's edge. We're not out of the woods yet.

I surge forward and join the effort. With my greater power, my unknotting has far greater reach than the others. With everyone's combined strength, we subdue the throbbing tangle. Finally, only a small bundle is left, and Tremor turns to me.

"We can handle it from here," she says, exhaustion coloring her voice. "The new elemental is almost ready to assume the role, and we can manage the rest of the knots."

"Good work, everyone," I say to the group, then I ascend with satisfaction. I managed my fundamental duties alongside my physical-world ones. I can do this, at least until Tremor and Quake are ready.

I open my eyes with a gasp. The dirt dome is intact, and a rush of pleasure fills my body. Sometimes it's good being the fundamental. I don't know that I would have had the power to make this dome otherwise.

With a flick of my hand, the dome collapses in a muddy heap. Instantly, a large shape flies toward me. I dodge the object and it flops to the ground beyond my feet.

My stomach contracts. It's the jogger, but the yellow lauvan that used to surround her body have vanished. Her eyes are wide and glassy, and her limbs splay at strange angles. She's dead, and it's my fault.

"I warned you," Todd screams at me. When I turn to him with murder in my heart, he blasts wind that sweeps me off my feet to land on the pavement full strides away. He turns and runs from the scene. It's only then that sirens reach my ears.

Alejandro skids to a stop at my side, panting and looking green from his injuries and the dead jogger.

"What happened?"

"I called Todd's bluff, and it wasn't a bluff." I swallow and look at Todd's retreating back. I need to chase him, but it's hard to move.

"Merlo, she's dead." Alejandro grips his hair. "I thought you were coming back to us. I thought you were remembering that you weren't a cold elemental. But this didn't have to happen. If you don't keep your humanity, what's the point of being human?"

A chill settles on me at Alejandro's words, but he doesn't know what catastrophe I prevented. Did it justify this young woman's death? I suppose we'll never know.

"I need to get Todd," I say and stand unsteadily. Todd is far away, but I can still reach him. I transform into a merlin falcon and flap hard until I'm directly above my former ally. With a release of strands, I land on his back in my human form, and we tumble to the sidewalk at an intersection.

"What's going on here?" A familiar female voice shouts out from a nearby police cruiser with flashing blue and red lights, but I ignore Kat Lee. Todd is within my grasp, and if I can subdue him, my task will be complete and justice executed for the innocent jogger. I can't bring her back to life—I never had that power—but I can make sure she is avenged.

Todd fights like a cornered rat. He rips at my skin, throws

139

wild punches at my face, and writhes under me. He's no match for my centuries of battle, and I bat away his advances with ease.

He changes tactics. Where before he focused on physical attacks, now his fingers grasp my lauvan. Damn. I've never encountered an opponent with my abilities. Before I can react, he yanks hard at the strands covering my face.

The pain is immense, and I recoil instinctively with a grunt. Todd wriggles out from under me and staggers away. I gather myself to follow, but a shout stops me in my tracks.

"Merry Lytton?" Kat screams.

Damn and double damn. Todd released my hold on my disguise. I must be wearing my usual face.

Kat pulls out her gun. Todd runs behind her for protection, his face gleeful at his close call.

"Put your hands up," Kat commands. Her partner mimics her stance with gun drawn. "Come quietly, Merry."

My brain flips through options with lightning speed. Transforming into a bird would be easiest, since it's near impossible to shoot a tiny moving target with a handgun. My fingers twist strands on their slow way up my body as I pretend to follow Kat's order, but the lauvan slither out of my grasp. Damn again. Todd's strand-yank must have rattled my body more than I thought.

Next—make a run for it. Unless Kat aims for my heart or head, I can heal any other wounds. And it's doubtful they would shoot an unarmed man running away. Just in case, I hastily weave an air barrier to deflect bullets. The strands are slippery and unwieldy, but I manage to construct a passable barrier. Here's hoping it will be enough.

I fake a lunge to the right, then throw myself left. Kat yells, and a shot rings out with a subsequent crunching noise as it hits pavement. Kat's partner shouts angrily at her to stop shooting. My feet take me in a zigzag pattern behind parked cars and trees, and shouting follows.

My goal is my motorbike, and it is luckily parked down the next street. I throw my leg over the seat, kick the machine into action, and roar past shouting Kat and her bewildered partner. She waves at him to get their cruiser, but I'm gone long before they can coordinate.

Sirens wail before I've traveled more than three blocks. I gun it and weave between cars, earning myself numerous angry honks.

I'm too conspicuous, and hiding is a better option than leading the police on a high-speed car chase. But where can I hide? My apartment is out, even if it weren't too far away. What's the closest safe house?

A street sign whips by, and I recall Anna's new basement suite. It's only a few blocks from here.

I take the next corner fast, then slow my speed to a leisurely crawl. I don't want to alert neighbors to my presence. Luckily, few people are out in this January drizzle, and the streets are deserted.

In the front yard of Anna's new place, a huge rhododendron leans over the sidewalk. I wheel my bike behind its ample foliage, position the kickstand down, and creep to the backyard. I don't know if Anna is home, but I can let myself in regardless.

My body aches from Todd's mistreatment of my strands and bruises from my falls to the pavement. I want a quiet place to lick my wounds and plan my next steps, although I honestly have no idea where to go from here. My best chance at catching Todd slipped through my fingers, and I don't know where to turn. I'll have to reach out to Wayne and the others. Alejandro crosses my mind, and I recall his injuries with guilt. I'll call him, too, and arrange to meet. He doesn't need to suffer for

141

longer than he must, not when I can fix him. At the thought of lauvan, I relax my own and let my disguise fall away. No one will see me within Anna's suite.

I turn the corner, and a blast of wind knocks me off my feet. My heart races as I scramble to gain my footing. How did Todd find me so quickly? He was on foot. I hid my lauvan in the network today, so he can't have tracked me that way.

I narrowly dodge another blast, and silver strands whisk by me in a stream of pummeling fury. My head whips around to my attacker.

A young woman glares at me. She's dressed in a black raincoat that almost hides her curves, and her mahogany hair is pulled back in a tight braid. Her attractive face is currently twisted in dislike, and her hands twist another ball of air strands in preparation.

My jaw drops. Is this woman another half-elemental? My eyes scan her strands and frown. She has three colors—elemental silver, human green, and a familiar human burgundy that I can't place—so perhaps she is possessed by an elemental. Damn it. I thought we had stopped that nonsense last year. And why the two human colors?

"Who the hell are you?" I shout as I dodge the next blast by rolling on the muddy ground. "Why are you attacking me?"

I don't hesitate. My fingers grasp the nearest earth lauvan and I yank. A wall of soil shoots upward, but the woman rises on a bed of air currents and lands in front of me. She wields two sharp-looking knives made purely of air threads. I admire them with curiosity and unease. I've never thought to try that.

"I want the grail," she says with a growl. The attempt at menace would be amusing coming from her high-pitched voice if those knives weren't so sharp. "I need it."

My blood runs cold at her words, and then it rises hot and angry. The grail in my pocket is the only way I can identify

142

Minnie when she comes back. It's my most prized possession, and there is no way I'll willingly hand it to this jumped-up elemental woman.

"Too bad," I snarl. "It's mine."

The woman grimaces then slashes at me with the knife in her right hand, but I have centuries of practice defending myself against knives. I dodge the blow then grab her wrist and twist until she drops the blade, which then dissolves into air. She nicks me with other blade, but I assemble a layer of hardened lauvan over my skin before it penetrates too deeply.

She retaliates with impressive speed and grabs air strands that exit my mouth. My lungs feel constrained, and I can't take a breath. My eyes widen involuntarily, but I throw myself into her to upset her balance. She topples over, and I trap her wrists beneath both of mine. She writhes with furious anger.

"I need to keep the balance," she shouts. "Artifacts are made with elemental power, and elementals don't belong in the physical world."

"Then what the hell are you doing here?"

"Caelus is the elemental in my body," she answers. "He's on a mission to destroy all artifacts then return to his plane. This arrangement is only temporary."

I blink in surprise. This woman sounds like she is in control of her body, and the elemental is simply a passenger. I have never heard of such an arrangement—in my limited experience, elementals tend to control a body during possession—and my curiosity about this woman grows tenfold. But then her words sink in, and I focus.

"Your elemental's mission is to separate the elemental and physical worlds?"

"Yes," she spits.

I release her wrists and climb off her. She rubs her arms and stares at me with a wary expression.

"I know that look," she says. "What are you thinking?"

I frown at her. How can she know any of my looks? I have never seen her before.

"It seems to me we're on the same side," I say. "I agree, the worlds should be far more separate than they are, and I'm in the process of transferring some of my elemental power to the other side, as well as cleaning up after another troublesome half-elemental."

"Is there any other kind?" she mutters. Louder, she says, "Then you'll give me the grail to destroy. It's a powerful elemental artifact."

"No," I say with finality. "I will not."

"Then we are at an impasse."

The woman raises her hands again for combat. I hold up my own palm.

"Wait. Let me finish." I swallow, thinking. This woman is a formidable foe, and I'm not convinced I would best her. What's more, she wants what I want. "I will not give you the grail yet."

"Yet?"

"I need it for now. My lover is promised to return to me, but in a different body. Without the grail, I can't wake her past memories of me, and she will be lost to me forever. I can't let that happen." I drum my fingers against my thigh. "If I promise to give you the grail once I find her, will that suffice? I want it for no other purpose."

The woman stares at me with narrowed eyes for a long moment. Her burgundy strands twist with indecision, and her eyes flick away to focus on something I can't see.

"That will suffice," she says finally. "If you swear."

"I swear on my life that you will receive the grail once I find who I'm looking for."

She nods and holds out her hand.

"Then give me your phone."

I pass it over wordlessly, and she types in her contact details before passing the device back. When I glance at my phone, the name "Morgan" accompanies her number.

"I'll be waiting," Morgan says. "Don't forget, or I'll come after you again. I know how to find you."

With that cryptic comment, she turns on her heel and disappears around the building. I lean against the house, drained by the confrontation. I could have lost the grail, and therefore Minnie, forever. Sweat beads my forehead at my close call.

I gather myself and walk to Anna's backyard. My feet take me down three steps to her door, and it's a matter of a minute to jiggle strands in the simple lock. I tentatively push the door open.

"Anna?" I call out. "Are you home?"

No one answers, and I slip inside and close the door with relief. At Anna's kitchen table, I sink onto a chair and begin the slow process of untangling my strands. I have had enough of knots today after the disturbance in the network, but my pain and disorientation won't leave unless I do something about it.

While I work, I consider my next moves. First, I need to make sure the grail is safe. I don't know Morgan at all, and I trust her even less. We have a deal, but how do I know she won't renege on it? The grail currently resides in my pocket, warded with lauvan, but I don't doubt that she could unravel my protections in an instant if she can see strands.

I put that sticky notion aside for a moment. How can I track Todd? I am really and truly stumped by this problem. When my wounds are healed sufficiently, I pull out my phone and text Wayne.

I lost Todd. How do we find him now?

There, issue delegated. I open a new message to Alejandro,

but my fingers stall. His last words to me still ring in my ears, accompanied by an image of the dead jogger. I'm trying to fulfill my duties the best I can in the final days of my fundamental role, but that means making sacrifices. Alejandro can't see that, and his condemnation pierces my heart. I can't embrace my humanity while I still hold fundamental power. I couldn't have made another choice, but did I even want to? Am I turning as cold as Alejandro accuses me of being?

I can't leave Alejandro to suffer with his injuries, no matter how little I want to text him after his words. He's my oldest friend, and he never lets me down.

I'm at Anna's. Come here in the next hour for healing. I don't know where I'll be next.

I lean back in the chair, exhausted in body and soul. Dead ends and impossible choices surround me at every turn.

One way to stop the impossible choices is to expedite the transfer of my fundamental nature. It's time to plug into the network again.

There are enough earth strands in this basement suite that I can descend into the network without bothering to go outside. It's cold and soggy out there. I lie on the floor and close my eyes.

When I slip out of my body, the weight of choices falls away and I feel calm and at peace. I'm not as soul-tired, and a part of me wonders what I'm thinking, giving this up. Do I really want to stop being a fundamental?

Then I remember that I can join the network anytime I want to, fundamental nature or no. All I need is my elemental self to plug in.

Heartened, I send a signal to summon Tremor and Quake. The sooner I transfer my power to them, the sooner my life will simplify. They arrive and greet me with pleasure.

"Ready for more stretching?" I ask.

146

"I was asking around," Tremor says. "And we don't have to wait until we're fully stretched to start transferring your powers. We did it all at once for you because time wasn't on our side, but the process can be more gradual in this case. The three of us will be connected until the process is complete, but it shouldn't affect our duties overly."

"Won't it make Earth less powerful?" Quake asks.

"A little," Tremor admits. "But we can pick up the slack. You should be finding your replacement for your fault line anyway, and then you'll have more time. You have started that process, haven't you?"

"I'm getting right on it," Quake mutters, and I try not to let my amusement show in my voice.

"All right, who's first?"

Quake and I push and prod at Tremor's strands, then Tremor and I do the same for Quake. They both appear more expansive, although the real stretching is not a visible thing. Their movements are looser as they test out their new forms.

"How do we transfer some of my power?" I ask. Tremor floats closer to me.

"Simply connect, and I will pull as much as I can hold into myself. Quake, you do it too."

Our strands touch, and Tremor's auburn fills my elemental senses, then Quake's loam-brown joins us. A gentle tugging pulls at my strands, then a strange feeling of release begins as power flows toward the other two elementals.

We stay in this position for a while—time is a difficult concept in the network—until the overwhelming presence of the other fundamentals joins us. Fire, Air, and Water surround our trio and form into their humanoid shapes. With a gradual release of pressure, Tremor and Quake detach themselves from me and flee the intimidating presences of the fundamentals.

I form my own lauvan into my human shape and face the

others. I feel strange, somehow lesser, after siphoning off a portion of my powers to the other two elementals. Far more than before, their presences are tangible to me as they float away, and I can tell exactly in which direction they are traveling and how far away they are. We are connected, just as Tremor predicted.

"What were you doing?" Water asks in a fluid voice.

"Creating a new Earth."

I have nothing to hide, no shame in my actions. This is the right move, and I'm pleased with the compromise. I can't give up my human side and devote myself fully to my duties, but I can't keep my humanity as a fundamental. This is the best solution.

"This is most irregular," Air whispers. "I don't know if I approve."

"I didn't realize I needed your permission," I say. Their censure emanates from them like I am a child in need of reprimand. "I might be new at this—indeed, I ask plenty of questions to best learn my role—but I am a fundamental. What's more, I am fifteen hundred years old, far older than Fire and Air, I don't doubt. I am your equal, and as such, I need the agency to make my own decisions. Please believe me when I say that my actions are the result of careful consideration and ample discussion with my elementals. I'm thinking of what is best for the balance of the world, and I believe there are others better suited to the job than me."

The others are silent, perhaps digesting my words.

"But two elementals?" Fire says eventually. "Never have two shared the burden of the fundamental role."

"Why not? Because if the only reason is that it's never been done, that's not good enough. Tremor and Quake work well together, and the transfer can happen far sooner with the power going to two instead of one. A lot less stretching, you see."

"Is it that terrible?" Air whispers. "Being a fundamental?"

"I can't let go of my human side, and I don't want to. I thought I could make it work, but I can't. I don't belong here. I'm too wrapped up in human emotion, and I don't want it any other way. Tremor and Quake are unfettered by humanity, and they will be able to make tough decisions for the betterment of the balance, ones that I find so difficult."

We are quiet for a moment. Water breaks the silence with a sigh.

"Your resignation from the fundamental role is probably for the best. It was a good choice in a bad situation, but involving a half-elemental was bound to end in misery. Half-elementals are a bad idea anyway."

"That's rich, coming from you," I mutter. Water was the father of Minnie, after he possessed a human body and met her mother.

"I know better than others," Water replies. "Half-elementals upset the balance, especially if the elemental parent isn't sent into half-dormancy, and of course any offspring the half-elemental produces must be terminated when they come of age. It's messy all around. This is why we banned inter-plane travel centuries ago."

My mind sticks on the word terminated. What did Water mean?

"What did you say? You kill children of half-elementals?" My mind races to my three children, all of whom died before their fifth birthdays. "Did you kill my children?"

CHAPTER XVI

Water's head tilts to look at me more closely.

"Yes, of course. Your offspring would have upset the balance. There is a set number of elementals that can be out of dormancy at one time. Elementals can't be created without sending some into dormancy, and as you and your children were not contributing to the workings of the elemental plane, they had to go. You had a special dispensation because your father submitted to a half-dormant state."

I feel strangely empty. Without the emotion that should race through my body, my mind is simply numb at the revelation.

"You killed my children," I say flatly.

"For the balance of the world? Yes, we did. I am sorry if that troubles you, but there was nothing else to be done. It was either that or kill you, and the previous Earth wished to keep you alive." Water sighs. "But that is long ago. With the transfer, we won't need to worry about your half-elemental status."

"I don't understand." My mind is still reeling from Water's casual acceptance of my children's murders, but I try to focus. "Why not?"

"Because your elemental strands will be fully transferred to your replacements. Your stands are now infused with fundamental power, and the world needs the future Earth to be fully powered."

"Also, it's much tidier," Fire says. "No fundamental in half-dormancy, and one fewer half-elemental to keep track of. You should survive the transfer process, but it's not a guarantee. Did you not know this before you started?"

"No. Wait, I might die?" All this information is coming too

fast at me. My brain can't keep up. "Wait. I thought my elemental strands couldn't be fully stripped away." I'm trying to feel angry, but my lack of physical emotion dampens my reaction. "Why couldn't we have transferred Minnie's elemental lauvan to Water and preserved her human life? Why did she have to die?"

"It wasn't an option." A hint of sorrow infuses Water's voice. "Minnie didn't have the fundamental power that you do, the strength your position infuses you with. It's only that borrowed strength that allows you the potential to survive. The process would have killed her regardless. I'm sorry."

"But could she have become a fundamental like I did?" My mind races over the possibilities.

The fundamentals glance at each other, and their consternation flows through the strands.

"It seemed cleaner to put her in a new body," Water says. "There wasn't time to consider options. In any event, turning her into a fundamental would have been fraught with risk."

"It was for the best," Air says. "You would have become even more incompatible than you were already becoming, as Earth and Water."

"I must go," Fire says suddenly. "A fire in Madagascar needs my urgent attention. Farewell, Earth."

The others take their leave, and I sit in shocked silence for a long moment. The fundamentals' appalling lack of concern for Minnie's old life shouldn't surprise me, given that they are not human, yet it still does. Then I shake myself. I can't lose sight of my goals, even with the revelations. I might lose my elemental side, but I can't lose the best part of me. Minnie didn't love my abilities with lauvan, she loved my humanity. If I lose that, then I have failed her. And since she's coming back to me, I need to be here for her, all of me.

Assuming I survive, that is.

I summon Tremor and Quake back to my side. They flow gently around me, clearly sensing my distress, but I don't talk about it with them. I need time to process it in the body I am comfortable in.

"Let's stretch and siphon a little more, if you can take it."

Tremor and Quake submit to their stretching. Halfway through another transfer, the draining power triggers my mind to whirl too quickly. Even without physical feeling, the pain and anger over my lost children threatens to overwhelm me. I can't push past the feeling anymore. I also need to check for Alejandro, since he will need healing. My threads disengage from the elementals.

"Until next time," I say without explanation and flow to my human lauvan.

I sit with a gasp. Alejandro and Jen are on either side of me, and they lean in with identical expressions of concern. Alejandro's face is drawn with pain, and his face is scuffed.

"What's going on?" Jen demands.

My breathing comes in shallow gasps as the full impact of my news washes over me. Memories hit me like punches to the gut. Mabelie, with her huge dark eyes and heart-squeezing giggles when I toss her in the air. Gisa, forever running too far from her mother Edith, but always returning for an embrace. My son Frix, proudly showing me a fish he caught in his first net. My eyes must be wild because both Jen and Alejandro sit back with haste.

"They killed them," I choke out. "The fundamentals killed my children to preserve the balance. Mabelie, Gisa, Frix. All dead before they'd had a chance to truly live. They have no idea what it did to us." I wheeze, unable to get enough air into my lungs. "I can't do this. I can't keep putting the balance over everything. I have to escape this role I was thrust into."

I find myself rocking back and forth, clutching my hair. My

skin crawls with the extremity of my emotion. It's not until Jen shakes my arm that I realize my unruly strands pluck at everything within their reach. Jen's hair stands on end, and Alejandro clutches the table to prevent it from soaring across the room.

"Merry," Jen says. "Merlin. Let go. Just let go."

With her words, her use of my true name, and her firm grip on my arm, the tears come. My body shakes with the renewal of grief that I buried with my children. They were in my life for a mere blink of my immortal eye, but the piece they carved out of my heart was immense, large enough that I couldn't bear trying for more. Through my anguish, as Jen squeezes me around my shoulders and I sob into her arm, I remember how each died. Tiny Mabelie swept away in a terrible flood. Feisty Gisa, her cries silenced in the fire so quickly. And dark-haired Frix, his little body tossed from a height by a wild gust of wind. None died from disease or human accident. All perished by the power of an elemental.

It takes a while to calm down. A fresh squeeze of pain grabs me when I think of the maternal anguish of Clotilde, Edith, and Gretchen, but finally my shuddering stops, and I take a deep breath. Jen rubs my back.

"I need to fix you," I say to Alejandro after I wipe my nose on the tissue Jen hands me. "You're hurt."

Alejandro shrugs, but the motion makes him wince. He grimaces.

"That would be good."

My fingers untwist the snarls at his side. Jen speaks in a hesitant voice.

"Merry? Alejandro told me a little bit, but what's really going on?"

I sigh and wrangle my thoughts.

"Todd got away again, killed someone in the process. That

153

one's on me." I carefully avoid Alejandro's eyes when I say this. "I'm preparing Tremor and Quake to take over my fundamental duties so I can separate the physical world and the elemental plane. Turns out that the process will strip my elemental strands off my body. I'll be human with no abilities."

My fingers pause at Alejandro's threads then resume their work. This healing won't be possible after the transfer is complete.

"Human?" Jen whispers. "You mean you won't be immortal? No finger-wiggling? Now you'll age like everyone else?"

"No healing," Alejandro adds with a wry smile. "I'll have to be more careful from now on."

"Fully human," I confirm. "With everything that entails. However, there's a chance I might not survive. It's a risk, but it's one I have to take." I finish Alejandro's side and move to the graze on his jaw. "I can't keep going like this. I'm losing myself. I don't want Minnie to return to a soulless husk. And it's the right thing to do. I'm an abomination, truly. I shouldn't exist, not of two worlds. My children wouldn't have died if I were human."

"Your children wouldn't have been born if you were human," Jen says sharply. "Don't wallow in guilt for something you can't change."

"You have no idea what you're saying."

"I have some inkling," she snaps. "I have memories of children in my past lives. Some died young. Sometimes I allowed it to break me, sometimes I forced myself to keep going." Her voice softens. "You can't change the past. All you can do is make the best choices you can, right now."

I finish teasing apart Alejandro's strands. He gazes at me and nods.

"Jen's right. Never forget them, but don't let your guilt over their deaths hold you back. Use it to propel you forward." He slaps his hands on the tiled floor. "What do we need to move forward?"

I take a deep breath and let it out slowly. Because they are youthful in this life, I sometimes forget that Alejandro and Jen have centuries of experience just like me, and their memories of their past lives grow sharper with every passing day. I will try to heed their advice, even if my heart feels ripped in two. There isn't much left of it to rip these days.

"You want my to-do list? All right. I need to transfer my powers to Tremor and Quake to remove my elemental side from the physical world."

"We need to stop Todd first," Jen reminds me. "You'll want your abilities for that."

"Yes, Todd." Another thought occurs to me. "I also need to keep the grail safe for when Minnie comes back. I had a visitor before you came. A woman attacked me—she called herself Morgan—and she was adamant that I give her the grail. She's possessed by an elemental but somehow has control over it."

"You didn't, did you?" Alejandro looks horrified.

"No, of course not. But I did agree to give it to her after I found Minnie. She is on a mission to destroy everything elemental in the physical world. We want the same thing."

"But you don't trust her," Jen says.

I shake my head.

"No. I don't know her from Eve. I must keep the grail out of her hands until Minnie arrives. Nothing else is an option. After that, I don't care what happens to the grail. I will help her destroy it if need be."

Jen claps her hands.

"Okay. We need to find Todd, protect the grail, and transfer your abilities to the elementals. We have a plan."

"That's not a plan." Amusement laces my voice. "That's a

list of objectives."

"Then let's make a plan," Alejandro says. "Finding Todd is difficult, but not impossible. Why don't you look in the lauvan network for unnatural fires, just like you did when Xenia brought her minions into our world? Then we can race to the spot and grab him. With enough of us, we can save innocents caught in the fires at the same time."

"Because that worked so well last time," I replied, but Alejandro's idea isn't a bad one. I can't track Todd's lauvan in the network, and I'm running out of places to look in the physical world, but even Todd can't hide a huge fire. "All right, it's not a bad plan. What do we do when we get near him?"

"Some sort of trap," Jen says. "Alejandro said you made a dome of dirt."

"As long as no civilians are trapped in there with him," I say with half a glance at my friend. "Perhaps this time I can make it out of stone to last longer. I'm nervous of what Ailu might do in retaliation, but we'll have to play that by ear. And I'll need to stay hidden. Kat Lee is still after me."

"I could meet with her," Alejandro says. "Make her understand who the real bad guy is here."

I shake my head.

"She's committed to her viewpoint. I'll simply keep my disguise until we find Todd."

"What will we do with Todd once we capture him?" Jen asks with a catch in her voice.

I gaze at her. She hates the killing in my past, but sometimes that's the only way.

"He might have to die," I say quietly.

"What if we stripped his elemental lauvan off?" Alejandro says. "Like you're going to do?"

"It will likely kill him," I say. "Since he doesn't have the strength of a fundamental. But perhaps it won't."

"Worth a try," Jen says firmly. "Better to have a small chance than none at all."

I nod my head in half-hearted agreement. Alejandro stares at me with an expectant look.

"What?" I ask finally.

"Aren't you going to check for Todd?" he says. "There's no time to waste."

"What are the chances that he's lighting a fire right now?" I raise my eyebrow in exasperation at my friend, but he only waves at me to continue. I sigh. "Fine, I'll check."

I dip into the network once more, but after a cursory soar over the city, I return to my body.

"Nothing right now."

"Come back to Alejandro's place," Jen says. "We can eat, and you can check the network every so often. If Todd doesn't light a fire tonight, maybe he will tomorrow."

CHAPTER XVII

Dreaming

A low moan escapes the hut. I continue pacing, too agitated to stay still. I've waited in breathless anticipation for armies to advance, for ambushes to burst forth, for executioner's blades to fall. Nothing compares to the agony of waiting for my wife to give birth.

Clotilde moans again, and I breathe deeply to calm myself. It doesn't work.

Ferrand, a village elder, shuffles by and glances at me. He must see my distraught face, for he stops with a kindly eye.

"She'll be all right," he says. His hand reaches out to pat me on the shoulder. "Women are stronger than you think. My Heloys gave me eight healthy children, and she's still around to bother me."

"I thought you had ten children," I say with surprise.

Ferrand shakes his head sadly.

"Erec and Jamette were from my first wife. She died in childbirth." At my stricken look, Ferrand belatedly realizes what he said. He gives me another pat, decidedly less encouraging than the first. "Clotilde is strong. You will have many years together, I'm sure."

Having dropped his pearls of wisdom, Ferrand carries on his way. I'm left more agitated than ever.

My feet move toward the hut when a cry of pain pierces the cool evening. Before I can enter the dwelling, a woman exits through the door and quickly shuts it. She turns to a bucket and dips the waiting ladle for a drink.

"What's happening?" I demand.

I don't know who is more likely to die: Clotilde from

childbirth, or myself from suspense. The woman chuckles, and the sound grates on my raw nerves.

"The usual." She wipes her mouth with her sleeve. "The pains take her, then they cease, then they take her again. She is progressing nicely. Soon enough she will push, then you will hold your little son in your hands."

"You know it will be a son?" I'm momentarily distracted by this knowledge. Does the midwife have some way of knowing? The tiny cluster of mauve strands on Clotilde's belly didn't give me any indication of sex.

The woman shrugs.

"No one truly knows until the babe is born. It's what we say to fathers while they wait. They seem to find comfort in hoping for a son."

Clotilde moans again, and the sound makes my stomach clench. I can't stay out here. I could ease her suffering in a moment.

"I need to go in there," I say and take a step toward the door.

The woman puts a firm hand on my chest.

"No men allowed," she says with a shake of her head. "It's bad luck."

"I don't care," I snarl.

"But Clotilde does. Remember what she wants. This is her trial to endure."

I stare at the woman for another moment then hang my head in defeat. Clotilde was insistent on tradition, even after I explained how I could reduce her pain with the lauvan.

"Fine," I say heavily. "But if she asks for my help, make sure you tell me."

The woman raises a disbelieving eyebrow, but she nods and disappears into the hut. I resume my pacing. I wish there were an enemy I could smite with my sword, but the thing causing Clotilde pain is also something precious. The contradiction makes my brain hurt. Clotilde is alone in her battle, and I can only hope that she is strong enough to win the fight.

An endless eon passes, and I wear away a narrow path in the dusty dirt before the hut. Clotilde's noises grow more pronounced, and women's voices make encouraging sounds, muffled through the door. Clotilde starts to cry between grunts of pain, and I waver in my resolution. I could rush in there right now and twist her strands to stop the pain. I might be chased out of town when my abilities are discovered, but it would be worth it to stop her anguish.

But then Clotilde would be under suspicion having consorted with a sorcerer. I can't risk putting her in danger. And what would they do to the baby of someone like me? My feet carry me on my well-worn path.

One huge cry from Clotilde galvanizes me, and I move toward the door. I don't care what happens tomorrow. This can't go on. My hand is on the door's plank when a new sound reaches my ears. I freeze. A tiny, coughing wail floats out, thready and high-pitched. The baby is born.

Shivers crawl over my skin. Clotilde did it. She gave birth to her baby.

Our baby.

I'm frozen in the same position for many minutes with my ears straining for more hints of what transpires inside. Finally, the door opens. The midwife looks up at me and beams.

"Méliau, come meet your daughter. Not a son, I'm sorry to say, but she's a healthy little creature."

I stare at the woman, my mind blank as her words rattle around the empty space. Finally, my limbs move of their own accord, and I push past her into the room.

The scent of blood lies heavy in the air, but the women are lifting soiled straw into a sheet and pulling to the doorway. Clotilde sits on a clean mat on the side of our small hut. Her

160

hair is loose and disheveled, and her flushed cheeks don't hide the pale of her weariness, but a glow of pride glimmers over her body with dancing lights of pale blue strands.

She looks up at my entrance. Her mouth smiles, and her eyes hold proud wonder.

"Méliau," she says. "Isn't little Mabelie beautiful?"

My eye travels from Clotilde's face to her breast, where a tiny pink creature clutches Clotilde amid the soft blanket my wife wove from lamb's wool last month. I walk closer and kneel, scarcely taking a breath. It's hard to image anything so tiny could be human. The baby's ear isn't much larger than my thumbnail, and a faint dusting of black hair coats her head with a layer of soft fuzz.

I reach out with hesitant fingers and touch her head. The baby's skin is softer than I imagined, and I'm afraid of being too rough. My calloused, coarse hands are better suited to a sword than a baby. Clotilde laughs softly.

"She won't break," she says with warmth. My fears must be written on my face. "Babies are tough. Look what she just went through."

Her voice shakes me out of my wonder, and I swiftly press my lips to Clotilde's forehead.

"Look what you just went through," I murmur against her hair. "I could have helped, you know."

"And risk that bad luck? No, we made it. Oh, see? Mabelie is looking at you."

I focus again on the baby. Her little pink cheeks face upward, and her deep blue eyes gaze at me. I feel exposed, as if she can see right through me, but it's not an unpleasant feeling.

"I always like trying new things," I say quietly and stroke Mabelie's cheek with the back of my finger. "It doesn't get much newer than this."

CHAPTER XVIII

Although I descend into the lauvan network every half hour until Jen finally makes me sleep, no flickering orange strands glow in the city. I sleep fitfully, rousing myself often to check, but there is still nothing. My dreams don't help, and the revelations of the day disturb my rest.

After a hurried breakfast that Jen glares at me to eat, I lie on the couch once more and close my eyes. The world of the lauvan shimmers before me in all its multi-hued glory. I gather my threads and float around the city, enjoying the cessation of throbbing emotions in my human body. Adrenaline, anger, and grief from the prodding of old wounds are fresh and raw in the physical world, but here I have peace.

Am I truly ready to give that peace up? What will my life be like without this sanctuary to retreat to? I didn't have it for years, but I have grown dependent on the relief from chaos. My conviction for releasing my fundamental duties wavers.

No, it's the right move. I hope I can convince myself of that.

Tremor and Quake are easy to sense, connected as we are, but I leave them be. I'm not here for stretching, I'm here for Todd, and I can let them carry out their usual duties without interrupting them for once.

I scan the city while I soar over glimmering threads of people, buildings, animals, and trees. A few fires catch my attention, but they are merely lights of candles and furnaces. If this were a city from my past, every home would have a hearth fire burning in winter. In this modern age, few houses contain a fireplace.

I float over the neighborhood terrorized by Todd, not expecting to see anything. It's not as if he lights a fire three times a day. Even he's not that foolish.

As I anticipated, the neighborhood is devoid of orange threads. I circle once and turn toward my body, ready to exit the network and return to my friends.

A flickering at the corner of my vision stops me. I twist to follow the movement. Sure enough, a small wriggle of orange strands eats into the brown threads of a building's corner. Although Todd's strands are hidden from me, I am certain he is there.

I memorize the location then race back to my body. I sit up with a gasp, and the others stare at me intently.

"Well?" Jen asks.

"He's there, I'm sure of it." I leap to my feet. "He just started a fire. Quick, we don't have long."

While we run out the door, I twist the strands on my face to change my looks. I'm a wanted man, after all, and Kat Lee is on the hunt. Catching Todd is more important than worrying about Kat, but I don't want the distraction of being hunted while I have a task to perform.

My motorbike isn't conspicuous enough to worry about, and I wheel it out of the backyard and sling my leg over the seat. Alejandro and Jen race to her Prius and follow my lead as I gun it down the side street to the main road.

The unfortunate neighborhood isn't far away, and it doesn't take us long to arrive, even after I dodge a few streets to avoid a police cruiser.

Burning wood and acrid paint fumes clog my nostrils with unpleasant scents. We must be close, and the fire is spreading quicker than I feared. Ailu must be on the job for the flames to be taking hold so swiftly.

I turn a corner and pull my bike to the side of the road. With a determined foot, I hit the kickstand, dismount, and lope forward. The fire at the side of the three-level apartment block is so new that fire engines haven't yet arrived, although a crowd of spectators and residents has formed on the opposite side of the street. Some hold phones up for videos of the spectacle, others hug each other with tears running down their cheeks. A few search the crowd with panic in their eyes.

Alejandro and Jen race to my side.

"I think there are still people in there," I say. "Look, some are looking for their kin."

"We need to get in there," Alejandro says firmly.

"Not without protection, you don't," I say.

With deft movements, I twist air strands around Alejandro's head then do the same for Jen.

"That will keep the smoke out," I say. "But it won't do anything for the heat. Be quick. I'll look for Todd and work on the lauvan side."

They nod with solemnity and dash toward the unburned front door. Before I begin my search for Todd, Anna trots up, panting.

"I came as quick as I could when Alejandro called us." Her mouth twists with uncertainty. "I convinced Wayne to stay away. I didn't know how he'd react to the fire. How can I help?"

Wayne's face will never recover his old looks from a fire attack a few months ago. Anna rises in my esteem at her concern for Wayne's welfare. Wordlessly, I weave the same pattern over Anna's face.

"To help your breathing. There are people still in the building. Stay safe."

Without an answer, she races to the building, whose whole side is one large conflagration. A strong breeze picks up and encourages the flames still higher. I shake my head and jog around the building. I need to slow the flames and sort out the imbalance, but stopping Todd is my priority. With him still on the loose, these fires will continue to be lit.

Finding Todd in this way feels fruitless, but it's the only recourse I have. I wouldn't doubt if he were long gone by now, but I still have to try.

I manage to skirt one half of the apartment block before even I can't put off my duties any longer. The fire engulfs nearly half of the building, and I still can't see my friends. Todd will have to wait.

I drop to my knees on the pavement and plunge my hands into the network. The silence is peaceful after the physical world's crackling fire and human screams. The lauvan knot isn't terrible, and it takes me mere moments to untangle it. As large as the fire is, it was lit only minutes ago. Ailu's infusion of wind blew it out of proportion and tangled the threads below, but it's nothing I can't handle.

I summon Tremor and Quake, and they appear within moments.

"Find Ailu," I say. "That air elemental must be nearby. He's probably hidden, but have a look around. We need to trap him and Todd both."

"We're on it," Quake says, and the two elementals zip away.

I ascend to my body and open my eyes. With a blast like a cannon, a fireball shoots out of the flaming building and ignites the house next door. Screams follow.

My eyes widen in horror. That fireball was the result of releasing the imbalance. It was my doing. Although it needed to be done, my stomach still writhes. Surely, everyone was out of the house. No one would be foolish enough to stay next to a burning building.

My thoughts drift to my friends, and my resolve hardens. I can slow this fire, although the balance might not be maintained. But if I meddle only a little, would that really cause a problem?

It's worth the risk.

I plunge my hands into earth strands again, but this time I stay in my body. With intense concentration, I force strands near the building to raise soil. With my extra power as a fundamental—even with some of it siphoned into Tremor and Quake—it's a simple matter to smother flames with mud. Extra energy from the tension of the former knot hasn't yet dissipated, and it's easy to weave into my working. Screams and cries follow my mud splatters against the glowing wall.

I throw more mud, again and again, and slowly the flames reduce despite blasts of air that must be from Ailu. I wonder how Tremor and Quake are managing. Wails of sirens in the distance alert me to the arrival of firefighters. Help is on the way.

"You!" Kat Lee races toward me, murder in her eyes. "I don't know how, but you're Merry Lytton, aren't you? You're not getting away this time. Caught at the scene of the crime!"

Anger flares in my chest, and I drop my disguise. There's no point if Kat has already recognized me.

"How many times must I explain myself?" I shout at her. "I'm trying to help. Or do you think mud smothered the fire by itself?" My heart gives a relieved flop when my friends emerge from the front door supporting residents of the apartment block. I point at them. "Look. My friends are rescuing people at great personal risk after I called them to help. How much evidence do you need?"

Kat glares at me.

"I need to take someone in," she says finally, a hint of pleading in her tone. "We need to solve this arson."

"Then take in the right man."

A flicker of familiar lauvan turns my head in disbelief. Can I be so lucky? Strands of orange, silver, and peach float around a tall man in the shadow of a tree's trunk. Todd's mouth is wide with his grin of satisfaction, and my stomach clenches in anger.

"There he is," I snarl. "If you're not going to take Todd down, then I will."

CHAPTER XIX

I sprint toward Todd, gathering threads in my wake with outstretched fingers. Halfway to my destination, Todd notices me. His grin slides off his face, and he conjures fire strands in his palms quicker than I can blink. I throw the random lauvan I collected at him as he tosses fireballs at my face.

Kat shouts in astonishment behind me. A small part of me is relieved that Todd outed his fire abilities in front of her, but the larger part is focused on our battle. I throw another random assortment of threads Todd's way, and he assembles a hasty air shield to protect himself.

But my blast is only a distraction. My real target is the ground under Todd. With as little force as possible—I'm ever mindful these days that my actions as fundamental have huge consequences, although far less now that Tremor and Quake have much of my power—I cool the ground.

Ice forms over puddles beside Todd, and he stares at them in disbelief. With a frown, he raises his arms to throw air strands at me. His movements are slow from an unnatural cold seeping up from the ground.

The strands he throws at me are sluggish and have none of the power of before. I smile grimly. Fire was right. I need to work within my element to thwart my enemy.

But I'm not done. Todd's face contorts and he raises his arms again, but flickers of fire on his palm are quickly extinguished by flesh-numbing cold. With a grunt of effort, I raise earth lauvan beside me.

Grinding and groaning are the only warning Todd has before molten bedrock, released from its frozen shackles, pours upward in a burning fountain. It encircles Todd in a dome once more, but this time, there is no escape. The dome seals completely. With another flick of my wrist, the lava solidifies into unbroken gray stone that steams slightly.

I'm not concerned about the heat that Todd is subject to. As a half-fire elemental, he is mostly impervious to high temperatures. All I feel is a sense of immense satisfaction and relief. Todd is finally captured, and the last task I need to do before I give up my elemental side is complete.

Kat skids to a halt at my side and looks between the steaming dome and me.

"What did you do?" she says in a faint voice.

I shrug.

"You saw his fireballs. I caught the arsonist. You're welcome. I assume that charges will be dropped against me."

Kat's eyes rake my face.

"We'll see," she says. "Nothing is clear to me. You're not off the suspect list yet, but I'll see about calling off the manhunt now that this man is in custody. Stay in town and available, otherwise you'll be my prime suspect again. You're sure this is the one?"

"One hundred percent."

Kat approaches the dome with trepidation. She reaches forward, then snatches her hand back from the hot stone.

"And how are we supposed to get him?"

"Jackhammer, I suppose. I'm sure you'll figure it out. Just be wary of him in there. I suggest you make a small hole and get him to stick his hands through for handcuffs. Shoot some pepper spray in the hole without warning. If you warn him, he might put up a barrier. Oh, he won't have many precautions for a Taser. Try that."

"Hit him with everything we've got, you're saying," Kat says dryly.

"Exactly. And keep his handcuffs on, even in lockup. He's dangerous."

169

"What kind of dangerous?"

"Dangerous like me." I give Kat a wolfish smile which she doesn't return.

I leave Kat to explain Todd and the dome to her colleagues. I will find Todd in jail and strip him of his strands there. A visit in the dead of night will give us the privacy needed. Security cameras are no match for my skills.

A pang of regret flashes through me at the thought of losing my abilities. I don't know how to function without them. My powers have been with me since I was a small child. What will I do without them?

I walk away slowly, pondering my future life and all it will entail. My musings are cut short by the arrival of three sooty people. Alejandro's black hair stands on end above his soot-smeared face, Anna's shirt is liberally dusted with black, and Jen's normally immaculate ponytail is in disarray.

"Success?" I ask.

Jen twists her mouth.

"We got a few people out, but three have severe burns. They're on their way to the hospital now."

"That fireball got the last one," Anna says. "I don't know where it came from."

My heart sinks. That fireball was me. I had to do it—otherwise, who knows what disaster might have occurred with the imbalance of Todd and Ailu's tangling—but that conclusion doesn't appease me as much as it used to. I don't want to make these choices anymore. I don't want to think only of the balance of the world. I'm not cut out for it. All I can think about is Minnie's reaction to the fireball injury.

"Are you hurt at all?" I ask the others to drown out my noisy thoughts.

Jen holds out her arm, where a nasty burn is red and blistered.

170

"Just me. A burning beam glanced my arm."

I shake my head as I deftly untangle her golden strands.

"You'll have scars from this, I'm afraid. Wayne can tell you my limitations when it comes to burns. You shouldn't have been that close to danger, you three. I thought you were smarter than that."

"There was a child," Jen protests. "A little girl who was too scared to move. You would have done the same."

I don't answer. I hope I would, but my actions of the past month as my fundamental nature crept over me like an advancing fungus have me wondering. Would my growing coldness have allowed me to save the little girl, if it meant that I would upset the balance? I don't know.

"What happened with Todd?" Alejandro says suddenly. "And why don't you have your disguise anymore?"

Anna glances around for onlookers, but I shake my head and allow myself a small grin.

"I caught the bastard. He's currently cooling his heels in a stone dome. Kat Lee saw the whole thing and said she'd try to call off the manhunt now that she has a new suspect. I'll sneak into the station tonight to strip his lauvan."

Alejandro beams, and Jen throws her arms around me in a hug once I release her now-flowing strands.

"It's done," Alejandro says with a lopsided grin. "No more arson. We can forget about that half-elemental pain in the ass."

"Now we only have one half-elemental pain in the ass to deal with," Jen says with a pointed look at me.

I chuckle, but my heart squeezes, Minnie was a half-elemental, too. Soon I will be the only one.

And then, not even me. I glance at my friends. I will soon join their ranks as a mortal human. My stomach flops with nerves, but excitement bubbles within me. I'm forever searching for new experiences to amuse my immortal self.

What could be more unique than mortality? New horizons beckon with a tantalizing glow.

"Is it eleven o'clock already?" Alejandro glances at his watch. "Merry, don't forget you're giving a class at Liam's school today at eleven-thirty. He's counting on you."

I don't even know what day it is today, let alone what I promised Liam. Teaching his students is the last thing I feel like doing right now. With Todd taken care of, all I want to do is enter the network and stretch Tremor and Quake. The sooner I prepare them for their fundamental role, the sooner I can move on. I wonder whether they had any luck trapping Ailu. I'll ask them the next time I enter the network.

"I've been a little busy, what with being on the run and all."

"That's why I reminded you," Alejandro says, not giving an inch. His eyes narrow in determination as if he knows what's going through my head. "You promised. It means a lot to Liam. Don't get cold on us again."

Jen looks at him quizzically, but I sigh.

"Yes, I'll be there. Luckily, I didn't get filthy like the rest of you. You look like you've been rolling in cold bonfire ashes. I should know, I've done it once or twice."

Alejandro chuckles.

"I remember."

I leave the others to clean up at their respective houses and hop onto my bike. My shoulders feel lighter already with Todd's removal from my life.

At Liam's school, I park in the loading zone. With a few tweaks of strands, the sign turns blank. I'll miss my little tricks when they're gone. Will I have to follow parking rules like everyone else? The thought doesn't thrill me. Being different has its perks.

Liam is setting out practice swords when I arrive. His dusky maroon strands twitch with his frazzled nerves, although he greets me with a façade of calm.

"Merry, you came. Thanks. I know you have a lot going on right now." He frowns. "Wait, I thought you would wear a disguise."

"My name's been cleared. Almost. We caught Todd."

Liam beams.

"Great news! Wow." He clears his throat. "Now, this is the second class with this group. They're the paying class, not the underprivileged teens who came yesterday. That was a wild ride! They seemed to have fun, though. This group coming today has learned basic handholds and blocks. I wanted to start them with—"

I hold up my hand to stop Liam's words.

"Liam. Can you guess how many people I have trained on the sword?"

He suppresses a smile.

"Countless," I continue. "You asked me to take over today, and I will do exactly that. Trust that your students are in good hands."

He laughs, and his strands loosen into flowing swirls.

"Okay, Merry. They're all yours. I have paperwork to do. I'll be in the back if you need me."

Within ten minutes, the students start to trickle in. I survey them with an aloof expression as they chatter and hang their coats on hooks at the front door. Most are wearing exercise clothes and look ready for a treadmill. I'm still in my jeans and tee shirt, smelling faintly of smoke. Considering most of my sword work in the past was done in full armor of various sorts—leather jerkins, quilted vests, or those despicable metal breastplates—mobility in jeans is not a concern.

The students form a loose cluster before me. They range in age from late teens to one hale sixty-year-old woman with a shirt that reads, "The older you get, the less a life-sentence is a

173

deterrent." They chatter for a minute, but when I only stare impassively at them, they eventually fall quiet. I let the silence billow and strengthen for effect.

"You want to learn how to use a sword." I don't frame it as a question. "The sword is an effective tool to destroy your enemies in a bloody, final way. It's also good exercise." The class titters nervously, not sure if I am joking. I'm not—the sword is a brutal yet effective way to kill—but they don't need to know that. The chuckles die when I don't react to them. "Not everyone will master the sword. But if you wish to excel, you will find no better teachers than Liam and those at this school."

I clap suddenly, and the class jumps.

"Choose a sword," I bark. "And a sparring partner. Today, we fight."

The students leap to their task, sufficiently cowed by my theatrics. I hide a smile. When they are arranged into two rows facing each other, I speak again.

"Mirror side, thrust forward. I know you haven't learned how yet, just mimic your favorite historical movie. Door side, block them."

Tentative swords jab forward, and the clash of steel rings in the room. I walk around, correcting wild swings and improving stances. The students are, almost without exception, rank beginners that remind me of seven-year-old boys I have taught in the past.

A young woman at the end narrows her eyes in concentration, and her black lauvan swirl in a steady rhythm around her blond head. She deftly blocks her opponent's wild thrust and steps out of her near-perfect form. I nod in appreciation.

"Nicely done. What's your name?"

"Nia," she says in a clear, low voice. Her cheeks are flushed with activity. Her gray eyes pierce mine, and she flashes me a

174

quick smile.

"I'm Nelson," her partner offers. I ignore him.

"Have you done this before?" I ask her.

"No."

She raises her sword again. Her ferocious determination strikes a chord in me, and I take Nelson's sword.

"You're clearly ready for the next lesson." I raise my voice. "Everyone, gather around. It's time to learn some offensive moves."

I demonstrate cuts and thrusts with Nia, who swiftly responds to my maneuvers with agility and a determination to learn. I eventually give Nelson back his sword and wander around the class, but my eyes frequently return to Nia's crisp movements.

At the end of class, Nia approaches me while the rest of the students shuffle into coats by the door.

"Thanks for the lesson," she says. Her hand brushes away a loose tendril that escaped her ponytail. "I learned a lot."

"You're doing very well. Tell me, what drew you to this class? Why sword fighting?"

Her forehead creases in thought.

"I was in a pretty bad place for a while," she says finally. "Then I had a close call, and it woke me up. I was tired of only half-living. When I saw an advertisement for this school, it sounded like the exact thing that would take me out of my comfort zone and engage me in the world."

"And are you sufficiently engaged?"

"So far, so good." She graces me with a half-smile and takes a step toward the door. "See you later."

Liam emerges from the back room after the students leave.

"Thanks so much for doing that, Merry. I really appreciate it. And I was taking notes on your teaching style." He grins. "You know how to hold a room captive, that's for sure."

"All in a day's work." I stretch my arms over my head. "That was invigorating. I feel so free now that I'm not a wanted man."

"Are you going back to the university on Monday?"

I shake my head.

"No. I have too much I need to do to bother with teaching classes. Besides, I don't know when my name will be fully cleared. I'm taking the break. Anyway, I don't know if the university is my future. Perhaps it's time for a career change after all this fundamental madness is over."

"I'm always looking for guest teachers. The pay's not great, not yet. But I keep beer in the back fridge."

I clap Liam on the back.

"That's why we get along so well."

I take my leave of Liam shortly after. I want to continue what I started, and that means stretching Tremor and Quake to take on more of the fundamental power. My motorbike carries me to Queen Elizabeth Park, and I find my favorite cedar tree with branches that sweep almost to the ground to provide a dry, private room beneath its canopy.

Before I enter the network, my fingers twist a barrier around the earth strands that surround me. My intent is to create protection for my body while I am incapacitated. The strands, however, feel slippery and difficult to manage.

I frown and pull harder, and they eventually morph into the shape I want. How strange. Am I not feeling well? Is it a function of the fundamental transfer? Perhaps that is throwing me off. I shake my head in exasperation and descend into the network.

Once summoned, Tremor and Quake float toward me rapidly. The sensation of their whereabouts is clear to me, connected as we are. When they arrive, I greet them.

"How fares Ailu?"

"Trapped," Quake says with satisfaction. "Ailu slipped up, and since we were watching closely, we got him. He's awaiting judgement from Air. Apparently, there's a typhoon that needs observing, but the fundamental will be along soon. I suspect Ailu will be sent to dormancy. At least, that's what I would do if I were a fundamental."

"Practicing your royal decrees already?" I tease.

"No need to practice. I'm a natural."

"Are we here to stretch?" Tremor interrupts our banter. "I have things to do."

"Ready when you are," Quake says, and he holds still while Tremor and I flit through his strands, pulling and stretching in a now-familiar motion.

It's not until Tremor is stretched and the two elementals are pulling energy from my strands that I feel it.

"What was that?"

Tremor stops her pull.

"Something's happening," she says finally. "To the north. Deep in the crust."

"We need to go," Quake says.

I follow the two elementals, bemused by how sure they are of the direction. I feel it too, but the sensation is hazier than it usually is, and the ever-present glow of nearby strands is dimmer than before. I have a hard time keeping up to the swift elementals before me.

We soar over the landscape of glowing strands until brown ends abruptly at an expanse of heaving blue. We float over the ocean, my sensation of unease growing as we travel closer to the issue.

Tremor dives into the tumultuous sapphire threads, and Quake and I follow. Deeper and deeper we sink until brown threads surround us once more. We drop deeper still, until the brown is laced with veins of orange. Tremor halts at a massive tangle of threads. Upon her arrival, two elementals sneak around the knot. They approach us and bring their distinctive flavors with them, one of freshly turned earth and the other a sulfurous scent.

"We've tried to untangle it," Sulfur says in a sheepish tone. "But it's getting too big for us."

"Are you new to this location?" Quake asks. They murmur affirmatives, and he sighs. "This is a recurring knot. Every few hundred years, it tangles and needs a fundamental to sort it out. Not to worry, Earth is here now."

The others emit waves of relief and back away to let us work.

"Let's get to it," I say.

We dive in and pull at the knots. I tackle a particularly large one to start. It should be straightforward—last week, I would have picked it apart with ease—but the release eludes me today. Finally, Quake sidles over, and together we wriggle it free.

I have no idea how long we work for, since time is meaningless in the network, but eventually only a few knots remain. Tremor beckons for the resident elementals to approach.

"You two can finish this up," she says. "We did the worst of it. Come on, Earth. Let's get you back to your body."

Quake and I follow Tremor to the surface of the heaving ocean, but partway up, every strand shifts around us. I stop.

"What was that?"

"The other elementals must have released the last knot," Tremor says. "It created an earthquake. Then one of those big waves. What are they called again?"

"A tsunami," Quake says with relish. "Happens every few hundred years at this site."

If I had a heart in this form, it would sink to my feet.

178

"Couldn't we have released the pressure more slowly? Why did we have to create a tsunami?"

Puzzlement emanates from the other two.

"There would always be a shock of release," Tremor says finally. "No matter how carefully we unknotted. A tsunami would always be created. There's nothing you can do about it."

"What if we contact Water?" I prepare my strands to send a signal to my fellow fundamental. "Water can slow the tsunami."

Quake circles me to get my attention.

"Water won't do anything. This is the natural order of things. If Water changed that, the balance would not be maintained."

"You are concerned about the humans affected by this tsunami," Tremor says. "Is that it?"

"Yes, of course." My strands twist together in my agitation. "A wave of destruction is traveling to shore, and it was my fault."

"Soon, it won't be," Tremor says quietly. "Soon, you won't have the responsibility of destruction in your hands. That power will rest with Quake and me."

It isn't much consolation, given that a tsunami will wreak havoc on the shoreline whether I am here or not, but the lifting of my fundamental burden does ease my mind. As a human, I can't make the tough decisions that need to be made. Elementals oversee the balance for a reason.

It's been hours since I last ate, and I'm starving when I arrive back at my apartment. I fry a few eggs and wait impatiently for my toast to cook under the broiler, then I shovel

179

the food into my mouth. My stomach finally satiated, I recline on the couch with my head on a pillow and my feet on the armrest. I'll relax here for a few hours, long enough for night to fully fall. Then I can deal with Todd in the peace of darkness. I know I need to strip Todd's elemental lauvan from him, but knowing it will likely kill him doesn't sit well. Todd feels too much like me but traveling a slightly different path.

But the greater good must prevail. Todd must be stopped, by any means necessary, then I can relinquish my powers to the new fundamentals who will execute their duties with far more objectivity than I can muster. I only hope I don't follow Todd down his mortal path too quickly.

CHAPTER XX

Dreaming

When Saturday dawns bright and sunny, with only a few fleecy clouds whisking across the sky, I drag Minnie out of the apartment and to Vancouver's seawall. She yawns until I shove a coffee in her hands, then we stroll along the still-quiet sidewalk.

Few are out at this hour. Mist trails in wispy streamers off the ocean, occasionally covering us with a blast of cold damp, but the blue sky directly overhead promises warmth in short order. The sea is calm today, and waves lap gently against the cement walls of the walkway.

Minnie takes a sip of her drink and tucks her fingers into my hand.

"I'm starting to feel more human now."

She brandishes the coffee cup at me, and I chuckle.

"Glad to hear it."

We're silent for another few steps.

"Not entirely, though," Minnie says. "Human, I mean. These changes, my elemental side coming through more and more strongly, I don't like it. I don't like who I'm becoming."

I squeeze her hand. There's not much I can say. Minnie is changing, and I don't know how to help. I would say I like whoever she is, but it's not entirely true. The bigger problem is, Minnie's new self doesn't like me much.

"I'm losing myself," she continues. "And the worst part is that when my elemental side takes over, I don't even care that my human side is slipping away. I'm scared that one day it will be gone forever, and the loss won't matter to me anymore."

"I'm here for you, no matter what."

Minnie flashes me a swift smile.

"I know. But I don't want it to get to that point. I don't want to be that person. I'll keep fighting. My humanity is worth keeping."

CHAPTER XXI

I awaken with a jolt in the dark of my living room. What time is it? I need to liberate Todd from his elemental strands before the sun rises and the police station grows too busy. It's simple enough to bamboozle a guard or two, but a busy station might be too much, even for me.

I pat my pockets until my phone materializes. The screen says it's four in the morning. I need to get going if I'm to do this tonight.

I throw on shoes and a coat then race out the door. Once outside, my fingers twist my strands in familiar patterns. They fumble a few times at the slippery threads, and I frown. Ever since I started transferring my fundamental powers to Tremor and Quake, I've had trouble with my strands. It terrifies me, if I'm being honest. Who am I without my abilities?

I force my fingers to complete their task, and my wings carry me into the sky. The cloying heaviness of the past few months has dissipated, leaving me with the familiar soaring ease of my winged form. I might be losing my fundamental powers, but the process is giving me back my airborne lightness.

For now, at least.

I transform into a human near the station's parking lot, then change my features with difficulty into an unremarkable man for the sake of security cameras. I hope my disguise holds. My strands are so slippery that I'm nervous about my abilities in a way I haven't been for centuries.

The front desk is occupied by one bored police officer who looks up with dull eyes at my entrance. Before he can react further, I stride forward and grab a handful of his lauvan over the counter. His eyes widen with fear and outrage, but I pour

183

my intention into the strands. It takes longer than usual, but eventually he slumps back in his chair and stares at the opposite wall.

I'm sweating—the act took far more effort than I've had to exert for centuries—but my goal was accomplished. With swift steps, I move past the desk and into the hallway beyond.

Detention cells are past a heavy door. Muttering drunks share benches with slumbering figures, but none has the tripartite strands I search for.

With only one empty cell left, my heart sinks. Although the door looks intact, traces of Todd's strands are draped over tiny cuts in the bars. I push the door open with one finger, and it swings forward, the bars around its locking mechanism sliced. Todd must have used his fire abilities to cut the metal with laser precision.

Todd is gone, and I have no other recourse to catch him.

My abilities are leaving me—my fumbling powers moments ago attest to that—and I can't deal with Todd without them. I am the hope of the elemental plane to manage Todd, and I have failed. How will balance be achieved with him running amok, free to ally with another elemental? How can I release my elemental abilities without having first dealt with him? I owe it to the elemental plane, and to the memory of Minnie, to defeat Todd before I relinquish my powers forever. But how can I find him now?

If there's one thing I've learned, it's that I can't do this alone.

A drunk yells obscenities at me as I pass, but I ignore him. In the hallway, I have bigger problems.

"How did you get back there?" The officer at the desk stands with a look of outrage. "Hey, Mike. Get out here!"

I dart past the counter as the officer pulls out his firearm. With a speed born of practice and necessity, I slam out of the

184

glass doors and into the darkness of pre-dawn.

Shouting follows me, but I turn into a side street and release my disguise with relief. Careful to slow my breathing, I tuck my hands in my pockets and saunter down the sidewalk. The police run past, and one stops me.

"Did you see a man run by? Light brown hair, your height?"

"Yes," I say with feigned surprise. "He went that way."

I point to the entrance of an alley, and the two take off in a sprint. My chest heaves with relief and a desire for more oxygen.

While my breathing slows, I consider the situation. Todd is on the loose once again. I was too late. He was in my grasp, but I didn't take my opportunity, and he slipped through my fingers like a wet fish. I dig my phone out of my pocket and dial Alejandro's number. It rings until voicemail clicks on. I hang up and try Jen, then Wayne, then Liam. No one answers.

It is only five in the morning. I suppose I can forgive them for not answering. I'll have to fly to Alejandro's and roust him out of bed instead.

At Alejandro and Liam's basement suite, I rap on the door. No one answers, so I fumble at the lock's lauvan and let myself in, intent on shaking my friends awake. I need to get Todd before he disappears forever.

Alejandro's door is open, and no one is in his bed. I frown. Where would he be this early in the morning? Perhaps he stayed the night at Jen's. I turn to Liam's room only to find the same situation.

I frown. One man gone, I could explain away. But two doesn't feel like a coincidence.

A sharp tug at my strands makes me gasp. Something is stirring in the network, and I am being called to help.

This basement suite has plenty of earth strands littering the floor, so I lie on my back on the living room rug and close my

185

eyes. If Alejandro or Liam come back, well, they've seen me do stranger things. They'll take it in stride.

"Earth," Tremor says when I join her in the elemental plane. "A fault line needs our attention. Quake and I aren't powerful enough yet to fix it on our own."

"Lead the way."

Tremor soars over the field of multicolored strands. I follow her so quickly that the colors blur together, but it's a struggle. She almost loses me once or twice and must circle around to make sure I still follow her.

My powers are leaving me, and a mixture of relief and terror prickles my mind when I think about the future. What will I be like? How will I live in a lauvan-less world? Assuming I continue to live, that is.

Before I have time to dwell on these questions, Tremor slows. Even with a scant third of my fundamental powers left, I still have enough to sense the pulse of angry knots deep in the Earth's crust.

"Earth," Quake says in relief. "It's not that bad, but it's just beyond our capabilities, even with the other two here." He indicates two earth elementals behind him, both hard at work on the tangle. "This knot is one of those recurring ones. With you here, it won't take long."

"Let's begin."

Tremor and I join Quake at the knot. It's a sticky one, but it's nothing we can't handle. Before long, the last knot snaps into place, and the strands flow freely once more. The elementals responsible for the fault line murmur their thanks and slip away. Before Tremor and Quake can leave for their own destinations, I stop them.

"Time for a stretch?" I say. "We're getting so close."

My need to find Todd wars with my desire to complete this transfer. With the lack of urgency that fewer emotions brings, stretching feels like a more important task.

"Yes," Quake says with decision. "The more power I get, the more competent I feel. When a problem like this one crops up, I'm annoyed that I can't do more. Before, I would have floated by without a care."

"Of course you would have," Tremor grumbles. "Greater responsibility will be good for you."

I don't answer, but amusement fills my conscious. They will be a good pair.

"Oh," Quake says in a tone of distress. "I forgot to mention in all the hubbub, but Ailu escaped. An air ally just told me. They have no idea how. He must have had help."

My heart sinks. First Todd, now Ailu? I have a shrewd suspicion I know who sprang Ailu from his elemental bonds.

"Todd's gone, too," I say. "Once we finish here, I'll find him, and do whatever is necessary to stop him. I was too careful last time. I learned my lesson."

"We will search for Ailu," Tremor says. "But if he hides his signature, there is little we can do."

I help stretch the two elementals, then I transfer more of my power to them. Not much remains, but still, they can't take everything I have yet. Full to bursting, they accompany me back to my body. It's just as well. I need to finish Todd before I hand over everything.

When I open my eyes with a gasp, the suite is still empty, although daylight now filters through the curtained windows. I sit up with a frown. I shouldn't have given away more of my powers. I'll need them to fight Todd. And where are my friends? My phone gives no indication that they have answered, although there is a recent text from a familiar number. My body stiffens. Why is Todd reaching out to me?

I have your friends. You let your human side hold you back too often. You shouldn't demean yourself to their level, you're

187

better than that. I'm stripping you of your burdens for your own good. Maybe it will remind you of your true nature, and how you shouldn't mess with me. You'll thank me later.

The text is accompanied by an image of a house with boarded-up windows and a padlock on the handle. A hand reaches from behind the camera. Todd's fingers spark with flames. His intent is clear.

My breath stops, then returns with shallow gasps. Todd has my friends, and he will burn them alive. Todd lured or captured Alejandro and Liam, and likely Jen and Wayne too. Maybe even Anna. My heart constricts. This is revenge for my attempts to capture him.

My strands rise with my agitation, but they don't create chaos around the room like they might have a week ago. They don't possess the strength anymore, and a chill snakes to my very core. How can I save my friends from Todd without my abilities? How can I defeat him if I'm too close to human?

My eyes scan the photo again, and my breath catches. I know that dilapidated house. It's on the corner of Smith and Bletchley, half-hidden from the road by a towering cedar hedge gone wild with neglect. I've only seen it from the air.

It's not far from here, perhaps ten blocks away, and I leap to my feet and burst out the front door. My fingers fumble at my strands to transform into a falcon, but they can't get purchase. I curse and try harder, but for every thread I grasp, another slips out of my fingers.

I've given so much of my elemental power to Tremor and Quake. Do I have any juice left to fight Todd? In a panic, I grasp earth lauvan at my feet and tug. Pebbles in the nearby gutter jump and shake, and my shoulders relax. Although my bird-form is too much for me, my abilities aren't entirely gone. I still have ammunition to take on Todd.

Ten blocks isn't far as the falcon flies, or even as the

188

motorbike roars, but by foot, the streets stretch like taffy. I'm puffing by the third block and sweating by the fifth. By the time I turn a corner onto the house's street, I'm winded and red-faced with my shirt sticking to my back. The street is a quiet cul-de-sac with copious trees leaning over the road, their naked branches reaching down like skeleton fingers. I jog to the unwieldy hedge and race through a gap in the foliage where a driveway used to pass.

Orange flames lick the corner of the house's sagging porch, lending a deceptively cozy glow to the hideous scene. Hammering from within the locked door and boarded windows is accompanied by shouts of fear and anger.

My friends are trapped in a burning building. I have to get them out.

My foot takes one step forward, then all my strands yank down. I fall to the ground, and without willing it, my conscious slides into the network.

Quake is there to greet me. Panic radiates from his threads.

"We need you here," he says. "We have to get this untangled, and it will take the full might of Earth. Tremor and I have much of the power, but not enough. Your piece is crucial to fixing this imbalance. I think Ailu and Todd's meddling has upset the balance too many times in this region. Quickly, now, or there will be severe repercussions."

He turns to float toward the nearby knot, but I stop him.

"Wait. I can't be here. My friends' lives are in danger, and I have to save them. See the flames?" I direct his attention to the burning building near us. "They will be burned alive if I don't stop it."

"I'm sorry, but until you have given up your fundamental powers, your duty is with the elemental plane." Quake's voice is compassionate but firm. "This crisis won't wait. If we don't solve it now, the eventual pressure release will shake the very

189

foundation of the elemental plane. Effects will be catastrophic. We'd be dealing with the aftermath for years." He pauses. "And your precious humans would suffer untold disasters of every description."

I stare at Quake's deep brown strands, then at the flickering orange of the house fire. If I help Quake with the earth crisis, my fundamental duties will be completed as promised, Minnie's memory will be honored, and the balance will remain intact. I will finish transferring the power to Tremor and Quake on our agreed-upon timeline, and my abdication will complete without a hitch.

But to do that, I must value the greater good over the lives of my friends.

Todd's words ring in my mind. Are my friends a burden? In the emotionless peace of the network, Todd's words hold a certain truth. I don't want to join Todd in his megalomaniacal schemes, but I also don't make promises lightly. When I took on the mantle of Earth, I promised to maintain the balance of the world, and I have done my best to do so. If I don't fulfill my end of the bargain, Minnie's sacrifice will have been in vain. Even in the network, my mind shies away from the pain of that statement.

My friends will surely be reborn, as they always are, and will have fulfilling lives with or without the knowledge of their past. I certainly have experience living without them. Minnie will return to me, and I will be secure in the knowledge that Alejandro and the rest will join the world as newborns in the future. Unless that doesn't hold true when I am no longer a half-elemental.

The orange flickering grows, and Quake's strands are agitated.

"Hurry," he urges. "We need to go."

I waver. Should I follow him? Some fragment of

knowledge of what my body's emotions would tell me trickles into my conscious. Alejandro's disappointed face stares at me in my mind's eye. I want to be someone better, someone like him. I don't want to lose my humanity.

I can't do it. I can't let them die.

Without warning, I flow into Quake and push out with all my might. He shouts in confusion, but I persevere. When I deem him stretched enough—as much as I can manage with the threat of fire flickering above me, brighter than before—I pour my fundamental power into him.

Quake's threads shudder at the influx of power, but I don't let up. It must all go, every last drop, if I'm to be free to save my friends. Tremor and Quake need to become Earth together, and they can only do that with all the fundamental power I used to possess.

"I can't hold any more," Quake shouts. "This is too fast. I won't be able to maintain the balance."

"Tremor!" I bellow while I send a signal to her through the network.

She appears, followed by a small host of earth elementals. Her agitation is evident from her jittery strands.

"What are you doing, Earth? We need you."

I don't reply. Instead, I glom onto her and pour my power into both. They shake uncontrollably, but even through my fading vision, I can tell that they don't have enough room for all the power. Neither of them is fully stretched.

In desperation, I reach out to the surrounding elementals and start pouring my power into them. One by one, they succumb to the flood of my strength. My vision fades as the last of my power filters into the elementals. Before I vanish from their world, I speak to Tremor and Quake for the last time.

"Thank you for everything. I know you will be much better

fundamentals than I was, even if your reign will be even more unorthodox. You will make the right decisions for the greater good, far better than I ever did."

Tremor and Quake are too occupied to answer, although I know they hear me. With one last faded glance at the elemental plane, the threads grow dark to me forevermore.

CHAPTER XXII

I blink rapidly at the ground from my hands-and-knees position. Nausea overwhelms my stomach, and I retch noisily on the ground between my hands. I breathe heavily, disgusted by the stink of vomit, then a crackling sound distracts me. I look up.

The dilapidated house squats forlornly before me, fire licking the second-floor windows and creeping along the roofline. My stomach heaves again, but I force my bile back down.

Everything is different. The world used to be covered by lauvan, and their loss is unnerving. Vertigo-inducing, truly. My brain struggles to make sense of what I'm seeing. Are my elemental lauvan gone? I glance at my hands, and the lack of any strands whatsoever nearly makes me hyperventilate. I sit back on my heels and try to take stock, but hammering on the door reminds me of my task here. My friends will be burned alive if I don't get my act together.

I stagger to my feet. It takes me a few tries to walk in the right direction. The visual cues I have lived with for centuries have disappeared, and it's as if my most important sense has been ripped from me. I'm being asked to conduct a symphony without hearing or taste a meal without a tongue.

The ground shivers underfoot, and the shouting rises in pitch. I wince and put one foot in front of the other. Although I have removed myself from the earth crisis below my feet, it is still occurring. Did I do the right thing? Are Tremor, Quake, and the other elementals working together to solve the crisis? Did that even work? Was my role as a fundamental the worst thing to happen to this world?

I have no control over the situation in the elemental plane

193

anymore. All I can do is save my friends from burning alive. Even that might be more than I'm currently capable of.

Another footstep, then another. My stomach roils with my brain's inability to make sense of my surroundings, and my entire body aches. It's getting worse. What is happening to me? Is the loss of my elemental strands killing me? How will I save my friends without being a liability instead?

Half of the porch has already collapsed from the flames, and searing heat blasts my side as I stumble across creaking boards. A stiff breeze whips the fire into taller peaks of flickering flame, and I wonder if Ailu is behind it. I have no way of knowing, now.

One glance at the padlock convinces me that the door is not an option. How else?

A boarded window on the cool side of the porch beckons. I cautiously walk to the other side, knowing I need to move faster, but afraid that I'll stumble if I run. My head pounds with the effort of rearranging everything I know about what the world looks like.

The board is fastened with nails as thick as pencils. I shake my head at the overzealous carpenter who hammered them in, then a voice screams hoarsely from inside.

"Jen?" I shout back. "Jen, are you in there? I'm getting you out."

"Merry!" Her faint voice shouts back. "Merry, help!"

No friendly lauvan sway around the wooden board. My grasping fingers have nothing to pull, nothing to pry. How can I get this board off?

Tools. I need tools. I look around frantically for anything I can use. The porch is empty, and the flames have almost reached the door. Damn it, I'm running out of time.

My unsteady feet carry me to the steps, and I trot down them. Moving is getting easier, as long as I ignore my roiling stomach and throbbing headache. A large, flat rock catches my eye, and I swoop to pick it up. I swallow hastily as vertigo threatens, then I race up the stairs as quickly as I can manage.

I shove the rock in a narrow gap between board and wall then pry with all my fading strength. It barely moves at all. Sweat beads on my forehead from heat, effort, and nerves. My fingers tremble, and my vision tunnels briefly. Is my body failing me?

"There are strands all over the board, holding it down," a female voice says behind me. "Why don't you move them first?"

I whirl around. Morgan stands behind me, a frown of confusion wreathing her face that is lit orange from the crackling fire.

"What are you doing here?" I say. "Never mind, it doesn't matter. I can't see strands anymore."

Her eyes widen.

"You're human now?" She glances off to the side, then nods in confirmation at something I can't see. "That's unexpected. Here, move over. My friend Anna is in there, and I'm not leaving her to die."

I step aside and she tears at the window as if sweeping away cobwebs, even flicking her fingers like she's dislodging spider strands.

"Okay, do your rock thing now," she says.

I don't waste time talking—sweat runs down my face from the heat of the fire—and I push the rock into the crack I found previously. The board budges a finger-span.

"He's getting the board off," Alejandro yells hoarsely from inside, his voice clearer now that the gap is wider. "Come on, help him."

I grit my teeth and push the rock further into the gap. With my foot on the wall, I pry the board with a grunt of effort. The board shudders with an impact from inside.

"Once more," Wayne shouts.

The rock slides in deeper, and I pull with a groan. With a screech of nails emerging from wood, the board loosens from its placement and falls outward. Too late, I realize that I'm on the wrong side.

With a thump, the board knocks me on my head and forces me to the porch floor. The already unstable porch gives way under my weight. My eyes widen and I land on my bottom on the dirt under the porch. The fall jars my back and clacks my teeth together to add more pain to my headache. I reach up to massage my lauvan, but no silky strands meet my questing fingers.

Right. I can't feel lauvan anymore. If I get hurt, I have to let my body do the healing. A chill races up my back. I've never felt more vulnerable. Do normal people feel this fragile all the time?

"Merlo," Alejandro calls down. "Get out of there. The fire is spreading."

Morgan reaches down a hand, and I clamber out of my splintery hole with many winces. Liam passes an unconscious Wayne to Alejandro over the windowsill. Jen and Anna climb out after, helped by Morgan, then they and Liam follow Alejandro and his burden. I limp along behind and skirt the intense fire of the burning building, whose flames are taking over the steps.

"I thought we were goners," Jen says with a squeeze around my middle. "Glad you were around to save the day."

I squeeze her back but don't respond. My "saving" was little more than a lucky break. The best I could muster was a jagged rock to help with. I never expected to feel this useless. Panic flickers at the thought of living like this from now on, assuming I will continue living. The aching in my body is quickly morphing to a steady throb, and I don't know if it's from my fall or if it's a bad reaction to removing my elemental strands. But it's too late to change my mind. How would I even contact the elemental plane?

Alejandro lowers Wayne to the soggy grass near the wild hedge then beckons me forward. Anna drops to the ground near Wayne's head.

"Smoke inhalation got to him," Alejandro says in a hoarse whisper. "Can you fix him up?"

I stare at Alejandro. Again, my uselessness is on full display.

"I can't," I say quietly. "I'm only human now."

Alejandro stares back, his eyes raking my face as if that will help him interpret my words. A tremor interrupts his perusal.

"And that is the consequence," I say. "I gave my fundamental powers to Tremor and Quake before they could handle it. I have no idea if they are managing or not. I would recommend staying outdoors until the earthquakes stop. There's a doozy of a knot down there."

The guilt of my relinquished duties squeezes my heart with a painful grip. But how could I have done anything else? Tremor and Quake's vibes of panic wash through my memory, and I swallow. I hope I did the right thing.

"Move over," Morgan says. "I can help."

I shuffle out of the way, and Morgan kneels beside Anna next to Wayne. With a frown of concentration, her fingers pull and twitch over invisible threads that I can't see. Is this what I've always looked like to others? How ridiculous.

I sway from a combination of vertigo and faintness from my body's trembling. Alejandro grabs my forearm with a strong grip and peers at me closely. He's mercifully distracted when Wayne coughs and opens bloodshot eyes.

"Who are you?" he murmurs.

Morgan exhales through her nose.

"You're welcome." To Anna she says, "Are you okay?"

"Yes," Anna whispers. "Thanks for coming."

The two embrace, and Wayne looks confused, as if he has never met Morgan before. Her connection to Anna explains what she was doing at Anna's place when she attacked me. I stand upright and glance around.

"I thought Todd would be here, enjoying the view," I say. "Why did you all come here, anyway?"

"He lured us here early this morning," Jen says with a frown of displeasure. "Sent us texts from an unknown number pretending to be you. He used our past names to prove himself. How did he know? I thought you hadn't told him details like that."

"He was the one who logged into our website," Wayne says after a cough to clear his throat. "He broke into the library and stole Anna's password."

Anna looks intensely guilty, and I scowl at the audacity of Todd using our past against us. I feel naked, somehow, knowing a relative stranger has skimmed through the bullet points of my life. Those notes were for my friends alone.

Alejandro turns to Jen to reassure himself that she is all right after their fiasco, and Liam surveys the burning building with concern. Wayne still sits on the ground next to Anna, looking dazed, and Morgan straightens her coat.

"If you're okay, Anna, I'll head off," she says with a swift glance at our group. She looks at the crackling building behind us before her keen eyes linger on my face. "When you're ready, you know how to find me."

I nod, the grail burning a hole in my coat pocket. With my elemental self stripped away, it's even more crucial that I hold onto the grail. Without even lauvan color to guide me, how else will I identify Minnie when she returns? A chill passes

198

over me. Will she be drawn to me anymore now that I am fully human?

Alejandro steps to my side as Morgan turns to leave.

"Do you want this?" Alejandro says quietly. He offers me my sword that was slung over his back in a scabbard he commissioned for me last month as a holiday gift. I think he hoped it would bring me back to myself. I kept the sword at his house because that's where we practice our sword work. I haven't done much of that lately.

My hands clench with longing. Now that I am so defenseless, having a sword at my side would be a tremendous comfort.

"Yes. Yes, I do."

I take the sword with trembling hands and strap it over my shoulder. It takes a few tries to adjust the buckle with my aching fingers. The familiar weight loosens muscles I didn't realize were tensed. Alejandro steps back to Jen, where she is coordinating the hunt for Todd.

"Let's get this bastard," she spits. "No one tries to fry me without repercussions."

"Here, here," Anna says. "But how are we going to get him?"

"Search pattern," Alejandro pipes up. "He might not be far. Spread out in different directions. The moment you see him, call the others and we'll come running."

It's a mark of how incensed they all are at their mistreatment at Todd's hands that no one objects, despite the danger Todd poses.

My phone rings, although it takes me a moment to realize what the sound is after all the uproar of before. I fumble in my pocket for my phone.

"Yes?"

"Merry?" Kat Lee's strident voice yells into my ear. "Todd

Holland escaped, and now he's sent manifestos to the mayor's office and news outlets. He says he's going to burn the city. What sort of danger are we in? Do you know where he might be?"

I close my eyes, this news hitting me in my already beleaguered gut. It's not enough to strip me of my friends. Todd wants to make a name for himself, force everyone to fear him—although he would call it respect—and stop hiding his powers. It's a beautiful dream, but I know from experience that telling the unprepared always ends in tears.

"I don't know where he is," I say hoarsely. "He just tried to burn my friends alive, but I got them out."

Kat swears eloquently.

"As for the danger," I continue. "Don't underestimate him. His ability to control fire and air is immense."

"Can we bring you on board to help?" Kat's normally strong voice has a hint of pleading. "We could use some of our own firepower to combat him."

My stomach twists. I have nothing to offer her, not anymore.

"Sorry," I say with true regret. "I'm out of juice, myself. I won't be any good to you. Good luck, Kat."

I sign off, my mood sinking faster than a tropical sun at dusk. What good am I anymore? Saving my friends from the burning house was a combination of a lucky break and help from Morgan.

A terrible groan, almost too low for human ears to catch, rumbles from deep in the earth. It's accompanied by a terrifying shift underfoot. I stumble sideways into Wayne as the ground continues to shiver like a horse dislodging a fly from its skin. He grabs my forearm with a tight grip. Anna shrieks with surprise.

"It's the elementals," I shout over the creaking of houses

and trees and rumbling from below. "They're releasing the pressure of the knot."

"This is supposed to happen?" Jen yells from her hands and knees as she holds herself steady.

"Yes, but don't be reassured. It might get worse before it gets better. Elementals aren't concerned about carnage in the physical world, only that the balance is maintained. And the knot was a bad one." *And I left them in a lurch*, I don't say out loud. Guilt twists my stomach from abandonment of my duties. Without my influence, how bad will the earthquake get? Did I doom this city?

My eyes travel around the frightened faces of my friends as they ride out the earthquake, and I can't find it in myself to regret my decision to save them. The cost of serving the greater good was too high for my humanity. I'm not self-sacrificing enough for that.

Pieces of burning debris fling outward from the flame-covered house behind us. Morgan stumbles back, her feet unsteady on the roiling ground. She has to dodge cracks in the driveway that have widened to crevasses. She slides to a stop next to Anna, and the two of them clasp hands while they wait for the shivering to end.

Finally, it does, but my struggling brain feels phantom movement for long moments after. Alejandro is the first to jump up.

"It's more important than ever to find Todd," he says. "The elementals have enough on their plate. Come on, choose a direction, and keep your phones on."

The rest follow Alejandro's natural authority. I regain my feet and trail after the rest, my vertigo reasserting itself and the throbbing in my body growing stronger. How can I search for anything when my view of the world is so hampered? I try to hold myself straight for the sake of the others. I don't want to be a liability, but it takes all my failing strength to muster the energy to follow the others.

"Wayne and Anna can go north," Alejandro says once we're on the road. Neighbors are milling around, looking lost and bewildered after the quake. One man examines his roof with a forlorn shake of his head. "Jen and I will go south, Liam west, and Merry east."

He glances at Morgan with a questioning look, and she shakes her head.

"This isn't my quest. Now that Anna's safe, I'm out."

She waves at Anna and walks east along the sidewalk, whose cracks are more pronounced now. Alejandro claps his hands.

"Okay, everyone, get moving."

I stride away from my friends in a passable impression of my former confidence, trying my best to walk in a straight line. Bile raises in my throat, but I swallow it down. My eyes scan every human form that passes my vision, but I can barely tell anyone apart. How can humans identify each other without the telltale glow of colored strands? Will I recognize Todd without his peach, silver, and orange threads? He's tall, I know that. Brown hair. What other features stand out?

Two blocks away from the burning house, the earth groans again. I drop to my knees, unable to withstand the jolt that rocks the world. People scream and race to the middle of the road, away from falling chimneys and dropping branches.

That's clever. I should move, too. I stumble to my feet and run a few steps. A crack makes me look up. A branch above me is growing bigger for some reason.

When it hits my shoulder, I realize too late that the branch was falling. Without visual cues from lauvan, I didn't realize it was in motion.

Agony explodes in my left arm and back, and I yell in pain.

The branch rolls off me, luckily—if one can call anything involving so much pain luck—and I drop to my knees, cradling my hurt arm with my good hand. It's all I can do to keep it steady while the earth calms from its incessant shaking.

What am I supposed to do now? I have no way to heal myself. What was I thinking, giving up my elemental side? My life is too tumultuous to not have healing abilities.

CHAPTER XXIII

"You big baby," a female voice murmurs. "Let me have a look."

Through a haze of pain, I squint up at the speaker. Morgan bends over my shoulder with her brow furrowed in concentration. With a few twitches of her fingers above my shoulder, the pain lessens marginally, and I can breathe again.

"Thank you," I gasp.

"It's not healed," she warns. "That would take too long, and I know you're on some grand mission. But you'll be able to think straight for now."

"I don't know what to do without my abilities," I whisper. It's an admission that I wouldn't speak to my friends—it feels shameful—but I don't care what Morgan thinks of me. Besides, she might understand better than most, given how she has abilities of her own.

An unreadable expression crosses her face. Is she trying not to smile, or is it frustration? Or perhaps both?

"Spare me the pity party," she says. "I doubt you're entirely useless without your magic. You still have eyes, two feet, mostly working hands. You have a sword on your back—do you know which end goes into the enemy? Magic is only one facet of your usefulness. Granted, it's a helpful one, but it's one that most people function just fine without. It's time to put on your big-boy pants and do what you set out to do."

I stare at my injured arm. Perhaps she's right. Have I leaned on my abilities too much? I'm formidable with a sword, I can best anyone with my bare hands—even without lauvan—and my long years of experience count for a lot in a fight or a chase. My mind churns into gear. Morgan's right. I don't have time for a pity party. I have to work with what I have.

I push myself to my feet with my good arm and survey the road through tunneling vision. A young child is crying in his mother's arms, an elderly woman wanders in the center of the road wearing slippers, and clusters of people look around in bewilderment, wondering what to do next. In the distance, sirens wail.

"Aren't you looking for someone?" Morgan says.

"Yes." I shake my head to clear it. "Yes. Thank you for your help. I have to keep looking."

My feet take me east along the center of the road. I circle around an abandoned car and leap over fallen branches. The motion nearly makes me vomit, but I push through the sensation. I'll never get used to this way of being if I don't push myself.

Another groan rumbles at the edge of my hearing, and I barely brace myself in time for the jolt. Screams erupt around me as the ground shakes far worse than before. Chimney bricks fall with thuds on grass, glass in windowpanes cracks and crashes in tinkling waterfalls, and whole houses creak under the strain of motion. Unable to handle the movement, a water main near the nearest fire hydrant bursts and sends a geyser of water into the air.

"Our house is on fire, Jason!" someone screams behind me.

I whip my head around at the sound. A young mother holding a baby with a young boy near her leg points at a bungalow three doors down. A man across the street, presumably Jason, wrings his hands. Perhaps the furnace broke apart, because the small dwelling has flames licking out the gaping holes of its broken windows.

A brisk breeze gusts out of nowhere, surprising me with its suddenness. I usually see air lauvan before I feel wind. The gust hits the house and makes the flames leap unnaturally high. Is this Ailu's doing? Is he using the earthquake's destruction to create his spectacle?

The little boy panics and runs with unsteady steps across the swaying street toward his father. His tiny body makes a small wave of wind as he passes next to me.

"Peyton, no!" the woman cries.

A crack alerts me to a breaking branch above. My heart hitches. A huge limb waves above us. The boy stops, looks up at the dangling branch, and freezes directly under it. The limb hangs for a brief, endless moment. With a final crack, it drops.

There is no time for thought, no time to acknowledge pain or my damaged arm. I dart forward, grab the boy's arm, and throw myself back. The boy lands against my chest, sending my bottom on a crash collision with the pavement. With a sickening thud, the branch collides with the ground and splinters into three pieces.

I clutch the boy's tiny body in my arms. His heart patters swiftly, like a frightened bird's. He takes one huge, shuddering breath, pauses, then releases it in an ear-splitting wail.

The quake has finally stopped, and the boy's parents dash to our side. They gather their child into a crushing group hug, and my lap feels colder than before. The warmth in my chest makes up for the loss. Terrible disasters happen, but they aren't my fault anymore. Now, I can do my best to clean up the aftermath and ignore the balance. Leave that to more level heads. I can act as I see fit and save whoever I can. Today it was only one child, but that child was everything to his parents.

This child's situation matched my own children's fates too closely. Nothing can change the outcome of their lives, but today, these parents will have their son. That will have to be enough.

The parents thank me with tearful gratitude and move to a part of the road without trees above them. Morgan approaches me with a wry smile.

"I told you so," she says. "Oh, that's a very satisfying phrase to say."

I open my mouth to retort, but another tremor starts. More cracking from the struggling trees above stops my heart in horror. From my seated position on the pavement, I have no mobility. I'm a sitting duck for any wayward branches.

Morgan stands straight and weaves her hands in a complex configuration like she's conducting a symphony. When branches rain down on us, they bounce off an invisible barrier and slide to the ground. Inside, we are unharmed.

My mouth drops open. The barrier really is astounding when one can't see the strands. I can understand now why people screamed "magic" at me for centuries. A pang of wistful regret hits me.

"Yes, it's a perk," Morgan says once the shaking calms and she releases her hold on the barrier. "You'll miss it, I have no doubt. But you've had your abilities for a good long while, I'm guessing. Time to pass the torch."

I open my mouth to reply, but Morgan's eyes widen, and she looks at my shoulder.

"Merry," a voice whispers.

I stiffen. I recognize that voice. My eyes search for him, but of course he's invisible to my fully human eyes.

"Ailu?"

"It's me," the air elemental in league with Todd replies. "I'm using the grail as a conduit. Handy, that you carry it in your pocket. Makes contacting you a breeze." Ailu wheezes with laughter. "Breeze, get it?"

"Excuse me if I can't summon the necessary mirth. What do you want? I'm busy stopping Todd from destroying my friends and this city. He has your assistance, I might add."

"Does it bother you, having me close and not being able to do a thing about it?" Ailu whispers. "Your powers are stripped

207

from you. How the mighty have fallen! You were once Earth, one of the fundamentals, one with power to move mountains and shift tectonic plates. And now, here you are, a lowly human. Nothing special about you at all."

My mouth is dry. I'm not sure how to respond. Everything Ailu says is true.

"Who's this bozo?" Morgan mutters, seemingly to herself. "Some rogue?"

"Things are rough in the network," Ailu continues in his breathy voice. "Your transfer was messy, to say the least. They struggle to contain the knot below us. You know what? I bet they'd take you back if you agree to continue your fundamental duties. Of course, after the debacle here, they'd insist on keeping your human side locked up for the safety of the elemental plane, but at least you'd have the power of Earth again. You left them in quite the lurch. I could tell them for you."

"What's in it for you?" My throat is raspy with strain. Ailu is giving me a chance to make up for my failures. I could join with Tremor and Quake once more, fix this earth matter, properly fulfill my duties, and pass the power to them in good time. But nothing comes for free.

"Lay off Todd," Ailu says. "He and I have a deal. We work together, he helps promote me to hurricane season. You chasing him crimps our plans. Lay off Todd forever, and I'll pass the word to your old earth allies."

My heart squeezes at the choice, but it's not truly a choice.

"I can't do that. I might have messed up with the earth elementals, but they need me to deal with Todd. I'm the only one who can, now. I might have messed up in the network, but a larger failure would be giving up my hunt for Todd. If it's the last thing I do, I will take him down."

"It might be the last thing you do," Ailu hisses.

I take a breath, but my lungs don't fill with air. My eyes widen, and my hands scrabble at my throat. Ailu is taking my air, and I'm helpless to stop it.

During our conversation, Morgan hasn't been idle. With a flick of her wrist, she throws something invisible over the area beside my shoulder. My lungs heave in a gasp of smoke-scented air, and I cough in relief. Morgan holds her hands together tightly, the strain clear on her face.

"I've got him, but not forever," she says. "If you want to find Todd, now's your chance."

I scramble to my feet.

"Thank you," I say to this enigmatic woman. She still seems so familiar, but I've never seen her before her attack on me the other day. She nods, the corner of her mouth twitching.

"You can thank me by bringing me that grail one day soon."

I run east, away from Morgan and trapped Ailu. I still need to find Todd, and with the delays, it seems more and more unlikely.

My phone rings. It's Jen.

"I see him!" she yells as soon as I answer. "He's heading north on Tahsis Street, right for you."

"On it," I say and hang up. My feet pound the pavement as I dodge cars, cracks, and branches. Huddles of people cluster in groups on clear parts of the sidewalk, away from the many leaking water mains. Sirens still wail in the distance, but the whole city is besieged by the effects of multiple earthquakes. The people here won't be helped for ages.

I'm getting used to the nausea, but my useless shoulder throbs incessantly despite Morgan's pain relief. I'm slow, so much slower now that I fight the failure of my muscles and my shaky balance. I grit my teeth and scan the street for Todd. Jen said he was coming this way. Surely, I can't miss him. Something has to go my way today. I might be dying, but I need to take down Todd before I do.

My heart jolts like the pavement did minutes ago. Todd's distinctive gait strides in my direction, two blocks away. Even without his tripartite strands, he's recognizable. His head turns this way and that to survey the damage, but he doesn't look distressed. If anything, he exudes calm. It must be nice to know one can fly away at any moment. My chest tightens. Never again will I transform into a merlin falcon and soar on silver currents of air. That's a blow.

Racing figures gain on sauntering Todd, and I squint to make them out. It's Alejandro, his face smeared with soot, and Jen with her long hair flying behind her. Todd must hear their pounding footsteps, for he turns to watch his pursuers. I transform my jog into the fastest sprint I can manage and pass an old man leaning against a tree who stares at me in amazement.

"What's your hurry, son?" he calls out.

I ignore him, because Todd raises his hands. I'm too far away for my shouts to make a difference, but I wordlessly yell anyway. Todd's fingers move, then two dust devils form under his hands. He raises his arms, and the dust devils swirl higher and higher. When they are as tall as the trees that line this quiet road, Todd clenches his fists.

Fireballs burst into flame at the center of each dust devil. Spectators, those who didn't back off at the first sign of wind, trip over each other to get away. The explosions settle, but if anything grow more ominous. Fire swirls inside each growing tornado, creating fiery funnels of hell-wind fueled by debris that litters the street.

I put my head down and run faster. Every step of my body inflicts my injured arm with stabbing pain, and my nausea only increases the faster I go, but I can't stop. Todd is right there, and he's attacking my friends. If I don't stop him, what was the point of saving them? What was the point of being a fundamental, and Minnie's sacrifice? What was the point of anything?

Jen screams when she narrowly dodges the relentless approach of a fire tornado. When I'm close enough for Todd to hear me, I yell for a distraction.

"Todd! Turn and face me, you coward!"

CHAPTER XXIV

Todd spins on his heel. His expression of shock quickly turns to exasperation.

"Merry. I was wondering if you'd turn up. I thought enough exposure to the elemental world would finally cure you of your human obsession. I guess you can't teach an old dog new tricks." He chuckles as if he's the first person to tell me that joke.

"I can't let you mess up the balance anymore," I say, trying to inject authority into my tone. The lack of my abilities is like a missing leg on a chair. I might appear to be standing, but one push and I'll tip over. I blink in a vain attempt to clear my tunneling vision and the accompanying headrush. "Stop before you don't have a choice."

"And what are you going to do about it?" he jeers. "It's my time, old man. The whole city knows it, now. After this show, no one will stand in my way."

He points to the sky, where two helicopters zoom toward our brightly lit section of street with their growing columns of fire. I shake my head, confused.

"I don't understand. What are those?"

"News helicopters." Todd looks smug. "I sent my manifesto to every news outlet in the city, telling them what I was planning. They're ready to film my big reveal. The earthquake is a perfect backdrop to what I'm going to do next. Everyone will think I made that happen, too. No more hiding in the shadows for me. No more being ashamed of what I am. It's time I was given some respect."

"This isn't how you earn respect."

"What would you know about it? You hide everything you do. Take some pride in yourself, man."

212

I have always hidden my abilities, but that never meant I wasn't proud of them. Now that they're gone, I do feel lost, but I'm slowly realizing there is more to me than my elemental powers. I wish I could tell Todd this, but I fear he's too far gone down the path that was almost mine.

Todd's eyes narrow as they rake over my body, then they widen. "Wait, where are your elemental lauvan?"

"I'm human now," I say with as much pride as I can muster despite the unease those words cause me. "That life is behind me."

Todd spits.

"You're a fool, Merry Lytton. All the power in the world, and you give it up to be nothing. Well, that makes my job easier." He raises his hands, and the two fire tornadoes turn from their pursuit of Jen and Alejandro to converge on me. "Since you're hellbent on stopping me, I'll get rid of you. I don't need Ailu to do it. I'm powerful enough as it is. Then, no one in the elemental plane can stop me, and no one in the human world will care what I do, except to treat me with the respect I deserve."

No one will care. Todd's words strengthen my resolve. That's why I saved my friends. What's the point of living without connection? Pity lances my heart for lonely Todd who has never had real friends. Perhaps his double-elemental nature leaves him incapable.

But pity won't stop me from doing what I need to do. Todd must be stopped—for the greater good, for my friends' sakes, for my promises, for Minnie, for myself—and it's up to me to do it, however I can.

But it won't be easy. I leap out of the way of a fire tornado barreling toward me. It whooshes past, then makes a tight turn to follow me once more. Meanwhile, the second twister is right behind. Todd laughs.

213

"Run, Merry. Run like the weakling you are."

Alejandro and Jen race toward Todd now that the crackling twisters are following me, but Todd summons two more fire tornadoes with a wave of his hands. The new ones chase after my friends. One passes too close to Alejandro, and his coat lights on fire. With a shout of shock, Alejandro dives to the side and rolls frantically to put out the flames before the twister comes back for him.

Wayne and Anna skid to a halt on a nearby road. Anna grips Wayne's hand, but his eyes are fixed on the four swirling towers of fire. His face still bears the misshapen scars of the burn he sustained during our previous elemental battle. Now, it looks like he is frozen with fear at the sight of fire.

Anna must come to the same conclusion, for she pushes him back, out of the way, and runs in herself to pull Jen from the tornado's path before it drops flaming debris on her head.

I dodge my own towering tornadoes before they crush me between them. The earth trembles again, and I lose my footing for one second too long. A twister catches my toe before I can throw myself to the side.

Heat envelops my foot, and I kick my shoe off in panic. My sock is half-burned away, and the skin underneath is red and tight. There is nothing I can do for the pain, nothing I can do to promote healing. I can't even douse fire with my abilities. Doubt creeps over me, even as the twisters double back and aim for me again. What was I thinking, giving up my powers? How can I survive without them?

A voice groans from my shoulder. Another elemental is contacting me through the grail, but this time, the deep voice reminds me of earth.

"Merry," it says. "Please come back. We need you. Take back the mantle of Earth. We can't hold on much longer."

I struggle to my feet. The burned sole is agony to stand on.

214

With my powers back, I could heal myself. With my powers, I could stop the tremors. With my powers, fire tornadoes would be simple to dissipate.

But with the powers of a fundamental, I wouldn't be able to disrupt the balance. I would have to leave my friends to their fate at Todd's hands. If I used my fundamental abilities—and they are inseparable from my old elemental side—the balance would be upset. An elemental must always act for the greater good. My friends would be at the mercy of Todd, and I wouldn't be able to intervene.

"Even the elementals want you to embrace your true nature," Todd's mocking voice calls out from a few strides away. Fire tornadoes illuminate his face with diabolical firelight. "Bet you wished you had your abilities now. Your friends are a weak source of power compared to the elements. Go on, be Earth again. I'll just finish up here. You won't be needing these deadweights anymore. Their deaths will strengthen my position with my audience." He waves at the helicopters then raises his hand.

He's right. I don't have any power here. All I have is my failing body, my tenuous humanity, and my loyal friends.

"I can't do this by myself," I scream to the others. My eyes glance between Jen, Alejandro, and Wayne. Liam has even arrived and stares at the tornadoes with dismay. "I need your help!"

Jen stares at me, then she screams. There is no trace of fear in her voice, only a vast primal rage that pierces my eardrums and my soul.

Alejandro shouts to join her, then the others. Todd whips his head around in confusion.

I've survived so long not because of my elemental powers, but because I can take opportunities when they arise. Quicker than a lightning strike, I leap forward, ignoring my agonizing foot, and raise my sword. Todd must see movement, for he twists back to face me with anger etched on his face.

He's too late. With one slice of my sword, his hand opens in a spurt of red. Todd shrieks his agony.

"A sword?" he gasps, clutching the stump of his arm to his chest.

"Power comes in many forms. Working together gives more strength that you could ever understand. And a blade cuts, no matter who the target is."

Todd's face twists in fury, and he wiggles the fingers of his intact hand. All four tornadoes rush together and form a fiery column almost the width of the road. It barrels down upon us, vast and crackling with burning fury. The heat and smoke are intense.

There is no escape. The tornado is too close. There is only one path forward.

With a powerful thrust, I slide the sword into Todd's chest. He has no weapon to parry with, and his only reaction is an expression of wide-eyed surprise. The last thing I see before the tornado arrives is Todd collapsing to the ground with my sword in his chest.

I close my eyes, bracing for the funnel of fire to envelop me in burning pain. I thought I might die from the fundamental powers leaving me, but I didn't anticipate ending my long life in the throes of a hellish gout of flames. My last thought, as burning agony rips into my arm, is of Minnie. I hope she is happy, in whatever life she currently has.

The heat that blasts my bare skin extinguishes. Cold air rushes to replace it. I open my eyes in confusion.

The fire tornado has disappeared, leaving only a swirl of ash that whisks away in a breeze. My shoulders slump with relief. Burns are a terrible injury, and without my healing abilities, I shudder to imagine the healing process if I had

216

survived.

Todd's limp body catches my eye, and my heart sinks. How had it come to this? I wish I could have reached him. I offered my hand in friendship, but something in him couldn't accept it. Perhaps we were too alike for comfort. I wish things had been different between us.

Jen limps toward me. Her breath sucks in when she sees Todd's body.

"Is he—"

She can't say the words. I nod.

"He is. It's over."

I tug my sword out of Todd's torso and wipe the blade on his pants, then I slide it into my back scabbard and scrub my face with my good hand. I avoid looking at the other one, whose nerve endings must be so ruined from fire that I can't feel the pain much. It's over. I dealt with Todd—my last true responsibility as Earth—and the weight is not on my shoulders anymore.

I frown. The earth hasn't trembled within the past minute. What's going on in the elemental plane? I have no way of knowing now.

The small, deep voice from before speaks at my shoulder once more, and I jump.

"Greetings," it says. "Earth wishes me to tell you that your teachings were heeded."

"Which teachings?"

"You intended for two elementals to become one fundamental, then you pushed your power into them and many other elementals. There was great confusion for a time. Then, when you said that you couldn't do this by yourself, the others understood the true meaning of your previous actions, and they realized you meant for them to join more than two together. Now, Earth is a fundamental collective with many elementals

217

working in concert. Thank you for teaching us a new way. Earth is now stable once more."

"You're welcome," I say in bemusement and shrug at Jen, who listens beside me. "I'm pleased my wise teachings were heeded."

Jen rolls her eyes at me and shakes her head at my arrogance. I grin back.

"I must leave now," the elemental says. "I do not want to upset the balance. This will be the last time you will hear from us. Goodbye, Merry Lytton."

"Farewell," I say, an odd lump in my throat.

Silence reigns from my shoulder, and I breathe a deep sigh of relief. It's over.

My friends slowly limp toward us. Wayne supports Liam, who holds his right foot off the ground.

"Broke it, I think," he says when I glance at the limb. "Hurts enough to be a break, anyway."

Alejandro's shirt is half-burned off, and his skin is red in patches. Jen examines the damage with a cluck of her tongue, then sucks in her breath at the sight of my mangled arm.

"Sorry, folks," I say. My arm is agony from the branch and burn, my head whirls with vertigo, and my body throbs from the removal of my elemental lauvan. It's no worse than before, and a faint hope surfaces that I might survive the transition. "I have no relief to dish out. We'll have to take a trip to the hospital like everyone else."

"Today, of all days?" Anna looks around at the carnage. Trees have toppled, chimney bricks lay splattered on the ground, pavement is cracked, and shellshocked residents crawl out from their hidey-holes. "Us and everyone else."

"Alejandro has a first-aid kit at his place," I say. "Come on. I might not have powers, but I've been a doctor in the past. I'm sure I can bandage us up sufficiently."

CHAPTER XXV
Dreaming

I adjust Frix's tiny hands around the fishing pole. He resists at first, then his fingers soften and allow me to help.

"Just like that," I say. "Now you'll have a firm grip when you catch the big one."

Frix's eyes light up at the thought, and he tightens his hands firmly on the pole. His eyes stare at the point where his fishing line enters the water.

I gaze at his determined face, his cheeks still round with early childhood, and my heart contracts. I ruffle his dark hair to distract myself from the feeling. He ducks his head to get away.

"Don't disturb the fish," he whispers loudly.

I chuckle and watch the line with him, but waiting is hard for a boy of only four summers.

"Will I be able to fish like you one day?" Frix asks.

I turn my head to study him. He looks up at me with hopeful eyes.

"I don't know. Perhaps. I didn't come into my abilities until I was about your age. We shall see."

"I hope so." Frix jiggles the fishing line. "I want to be like you. I want to do things like you do."

I heave a sigh. I have no idea what I want for Frix. If he develops his own abilities, he will be able to defend himself, which is something any parent hopes for. But that would also mean he would be in greater danger from those who are small-minded about magic. And would he have immortality like me? A companion of my blood would be a dream for me, but I don't know that I would wish my fate on anyone else.

"You have a pretty amazing father, I understand." I grin at him then sober. "But I would rather you inherit your mother's loving nature and open-mindedness instead. There are more important abilities than magic powers."

I burst through our front door and slam it shut behind me. The rickety timber dwelling rattles ominously.

"Edith!" I call out. "Where are you?"

My wife Edith emerges from the sleeping quarters with our daughter Gisa on her hip. She stands beside the table with a question in her warm brown eyes.

"Papa." Gisa holds her arms out for me to take her, but I don't reach for the little girl. Instead, I grab a sack that hangs beside the door and start unhooking cured meats and ropes of onions from the ceiling to throw inside.

"Sorry, sweeting," I tell her. "Papa needs to pack." To Edith, I say, "I've been found out, and there were too many to confuse. They'll be after us shortly."

To her credit, Edith immediately puts Gisa down and rushes to grab a sack of her own.

"What happened?" she asks as she puts a cooking pot in her sack.

"The blacksmith Supplice was severely burned. He would have died if I hadn't helped, but of course his elderly father saw my handwaving and Supplice's miraculous recovery." I roll our woven blanket into a rough bundle and shove it in my sack. "Before I could stop him and modify his memory, he ran into the street and started hollering that I was a sorcerer."

Edith's mouth is set in a grim line. Gisa wanders toward me and gazes up with her big eyes wide.

"Is sorcerer bad?" she asks.

I sigh and bend down to look her in the eye.

"Not bad, just different. People get scared by different, sometimes."

"I like your different," she says.

I press a kiss on her forehead. Edith ties the strap of her sack closed.

"Different is exciting," she says firmly. "And we will be starting a different life today." She smiles at me, that heart-stopping smile that I never tire of. "Let's go on an adventure. This town was getting dull. It's time to try something new."

It's a brilliant spring day, and I find myself whistling as I walk. The dirt path on this gently rolling hillside is firm underfoot thanks to a recent dry spell, and walking is easy.

I have no firm destination, but it's too pleasant this morning to care. Cattle graze on the slope nearby, munching on their cud, and a small cowherd lies on his back, staring at fleecy clouds that float lazily across the sky. An abandoned hut perches on an outcrop, but even its dilapidated state with its thatched roof caved in looks picturesque to my eyes.

I am content, and it isn't often I claim that. With surprise, I wonder if I have finally moved on from the death of Clotilde. A small ache presents itself in my heart, but it fades when I rub my chest. Another ache appears at the memory of little Mabelie, but the wound has healed over. Scars remain—they will forever be emblazoned on my soul—but the wound no longer bleeds freely.

I release a deep sigh. If I'm content for once, I won't second-guess myself. I wonder if I will meet another woman one day, another lover who reaches deep and doesn't let go. I think I'm finally ready for her.

I crest another hill and gaze at the sight below. A small cluster of houses, perhaps a few dozen in total, lies on the banks of a slow-moving river that winds between umbrella-like willows and disappears behind the next hill. The houses are thatched with golden straw, and chickens peck at their thresholds.

The wind carries laughter and happy shouts to my vantage, and I peer closer. At the village's central clearing, a tall pole made from a straight tree trunk is covered with strips of colored cloth and garlands of spring flowers. Figures dance around it to the faint pulse of a drum, and I smile.

Spring is a time of new beginnings and fresh starts. I walk briskly down the path toward the maypole. If I'm lucky, a bright-eyed beauty will let me dance with her. I'm ready to meet my future.

CHAPTER XXVI

Two months later

I shove a loaf of bread into my backpack next to a bottle of wine and some camembert. I tuck my phone more securely between my shoulder and ear while I rummage in the fridge for the grapes I'm sure I bought yesterday.

"Hola, Merlo. Have you booked the rental van for next weekend?" Alejandro's voice chirps in my ear. "I have twelve people signed up for our first adventure hike. The sliding pay scale really helped open it up to people. Your investment into the business made it possible."

"Is it an investment if I'm part owner?"

"I guess not. I think it's going to be big, though. We're going to help so many people. There's something about braving the elements that really brings out people's true nature."

I smile to myself. Alejandro's enthusiasm is always infectious. He cares so much for these lonely strangers, and I can't help but care as well. A shiver crosses my shoulders at how close I came to cutting all ties with my human side. My humanity is a vital part of me, and now I can follow Alejandro's lead on how best to use it.

"The vans are available," I say. "I'll book one tomorrow. But now, I'm due to take Nia on a hike."

"Yeah, yeah. Woman first, I get it."

"Damn straight," Jen's voice calls out in the background.

"Later, Merlo."

"See you tomorrow."

When my picnic is packed, I sling the backpack on my back, careful to avoid brushing the still-tender burn on my arm, and stride toward the door. The bathroom mirror catches my eye. I frown and walk closer. Is that a gray hair at my temple?

I prod the offending strand with a curious finger, then I smile. I'm fully human now. Every experience is now mine to embrace. It's a whole new world, and I always crave novelty.

It's a crisp day in April, and the skies are a clear blue. Even the sun shines with a modicum of warmth. Nia waits for me outside her tidy apartment with flower boxes on every windowsill. She jogs to my motorbike when it growls to a halt.

"Hey, you," she says with a bright smile. Her coat is open with the unseasonable warmth, and her curve-hugging shirt is on display. I can't help smiling back.

"Hey, yourself. Ready to put some power between your legs?"

Nia chuckles.

"You're so rude. But yes, I sure am." She pulls something flat out of her pocket, peels off a sticker, and slaps it on my new spare helmet. "There. Now you'll know it's mine."

The sticker is of a large wave from a local surf shop. I stare at it for a long moment. Nia and I have been dating for a few weeks, and she is sneaking her way into my heart. I haven't given her the grail to touch yet, mainly because I'm a coward—what if she's not Minnie and I have to give up the company of this beautiful woman in my endless quest for my soulmate? Her strands, when I could see them, were black, but I didn't get a close look. What if they were the darkest blue?

I can't handle the desperate search for Minnie. I have to either accept that she will gravitate to me in her own time, or allow myself to exist in a yearning, driven state.

I think I'm almost ready, though. Today, we're hiking to Minnie's lake. I haven't told Nia anything about Minnie or my past, but I did bring the grail along. Just in case.

Her helmet sticker is one more clue to her identity. I hope

224

I'm not reading too much into it.

"Marking your territory, are you?" I raise an eyebrow, and Nia laughs.

"You know it."

She swings her leg over the back saddle. Once her arms snake around my stomach with welcome warmth, I push away from the curb and point my wheels toward the mountains.

We can't talk while we ride, so I bask in the contentment of a woman's arms around me and the simplicity of my life right now. My responsibilities are to my new business with Alejandro, not to the entire Earth. I am not torn between two worlds. Without abilities, I'm as grounded in humanity as I can possibly be. The aches of my fundamental strands being ripped away from me dissipated after a week, to my intense relief. I have finally adjusted to not seeing lauvan everywhere I look, and although I miss it, the loss grows less with every passing day.

The past is where it belongs, the future is uncertain but hopeful, and the present is comfortable. I have a new purpose with Alejandro, but it's not one that I cling to like a lifeline, the way I did with my fundamental duties. I am content, and that's a very foreign sensation that I look forward to getting used to.

We pull into a parking lot on Cypress Mountain, and I kill the engine. Nia hops off the bike and pulls the helmet off with an accompanying shake of her thick blond hair. She sees me watching and hams it up, pretending to swing her hair around like a shampoo commercial. I chuckle.

"I see whatever product you're using is working."

She laughs and hands me her helmet, then she spots a young family across the parking lot. A toddler walks unsteadily behind his family's van until his father swoops him up and stands him in the van's back hatch with a laughing admonishment.

"What a cutie," she says. "I'm totally not ready for that yet, but one day." She laughs again. "Not the sort of thing you want to hear from your date, is it? Oh, well. I've never been accused of being subtle."

"I'd rather hear your mind than what you think I want to hear." I consider the father, who is now trying to wrestle a hat on the toddler with bear growls that make the little boy giggle uncontrollably. I slide my hand into Nia's. "Maybe one day."

She pulls me toward the trailhead, but I squeeze her hand and let go.

"Give me a moment," I say. "I have a quick text to send."

I open my messaging app and click on Morgan's number.

I might be ready to give you the grail tomorrow. I'll let you know.

ALSO BY EMMA SHELFORD

Magical Morgan
Daughters of Dusk
Mothers of Mist
Elders of Ether

Immortal Merlin
Ignition
Winded
Floodgates
Buried
Possessed
Unleashed
Worshiped
Unraveled

Nautilus Legends
Free Dive
Caught
Surfacing

Breenan Series
Mark of the Breenan
Garden of Last Hope
Realm of the Forgotten

ACKNOWLEDGEMENTS

Thank you for my wonderful reading team: Wendy Callendar, Steven Shelford, Dave Roche, Cat Kennedy, and Anna McCluskey. Deranged Doctor Designs produced a gorgeous cover for the series finale.

ABOUT THE AUTHOR

Emma Shelford feels that life is only complete with healthy doses of magic, history, and science. Since these aren't often found in the same place, she creates her own worlds where they happily coexist. If you catch her in person, she will eagerly discuss Lord of the Rings ad nauseam, why the ancient Sumerians are so cool, and the important role of phytoplankton in the ocean.

Emma is the author of multiple urban fantasy series, including Magical Morgan, Immortal Merlin, Nautilus Legends, and the Breenan Series.

Printed in Great Britain
by Amazon

80840464R00140